Man Overboard . . .

Yawning, he watched the dark figure standing ahead of him on the narrow promenade.

There was something . . .

Longarm flattened himself against a doorway to one of the staterooms and pulled his .45 seconds ahead of another snap and flash from the hand of the unknown person in the shadows.

His Colt thundered, the sound of it completely overpowering that of the small-caliber revolver at the far end of the deck.

Longarm heard the dull, meaty thud of lead striking flesh, and a man's form detached itself from the shadows.

He stepped out in plain sight, so Longarm shot the son of a bitch again.

The man grunted, spun halfway around to his left, and fell over the railing onto the churning sidewheel paddles.

Within seconds he was gone, driven underneath the dark waters of the Missouri by the turning wheel, silvery in the moonlight.

→TABOR EVANS→

LONGARM

AND THE
WHISKEY RUNNERS

JOVE BOOKS, NEW YORK

BERKLEY PUBLISHING GROUP
Published by the Penguin Group
Penguin Group (USA) LLC
375 Hudson Street, New York, New York 10014

USA • Canada • UK • Ireland • Australia • New Zealand • India • South Africa • China

penguin.com

A Penguin Random House Company

LONGARM AND THE WHISKEY RUNNERS

A Jove Book / published by arrangement with the author

For information, address: The Berkley Publishing Group,
a division of Penguin Group (USA) LLC,
375 Hudson Street, New York, New York 10014.

ISBN: 978-0-515-15486-3

PUBLISHING HISTORY
Jove mass-market edition / November 2014

PRINTED IN THE UNITED STATES OF AMERICA

10 9 8 7 6 5 4 3 2 1

Cover illustration by Milo Sinovcic.

Chapter 1

"You took your sweet time at lunch, Long," the boss complained when the tall man known as Longarm—as in "the long arm of the law" . . . and other meanings—entered the office of the United States marshal for the Denver District.

"Henry said there wasn't much happenin', Billy," Longarm said to Marshal Billy Vail as Longarm draped his flat-crowned, snuff brown Stetson onto one of the arms of the hat rack that stood beside the door to the boss's private office.

"When you left, I suppose there wasn't," Vail conceded, "but we've gotten the mail since then. Something came up."

"Oh?" Deputy Marshal Custis Long glanced across the room at Vail's clerk, Henry, giving the bespectacled and overworked clerk a suspicious look as if the incomplete information were somehow Henry's fault. "An' what would that be? Not more papers t' serve, I hope. I am heartily sick o' serving warrants."

"No, no papers to serve. Come into my office. We'll talk about it." Vail motioned Longarm ahead of him into the office on the first floor of Denver's Federal Building on Colfax Avenue.

Longarm passed through the doorway, a big man, over six feet in height with brown hair and a huge sweep of seal brown handlebar mustache. He had golden brown eyes that could on occasion turn cold as ice, chiseled features that women tended to find attractive, and a horseman's lean build.

He wore a brown tweed coat, checkered black-and-white trousers, a calfskin vest, and black calf-high cavalry boots. Matching that black leather was a gun belt with a double-action .45 caliber Colt revolver carried high and to the left of his belt buckle in a cross-draw rig. In the watch pocket in his vest, Longarm carried a .41 caliber derringer pistol.

By long habit he took a seat in one of the chairs set facing Billy Vail's broad, gleamingly polished desk.

Vail came around to the other side of the desk and seated himself in his comfortable swivel chair. Billy leaned back, the springs under the chair creaking loudly, and paused for a moment, steepling his hands beneath his chin.

The boss had a round face, red complexion, and was bald as the proverbial boiled egg. He looked like a man who had spent his life pushing papers around the top of a desk. In fact, Billy Vail was salty. A former Texas Ranger, he had smelled more than his share of gun smoke. There was not a thing he could ask one of his deputies to do that he would not have been perfectly capable of handling himself.

His cadre of deputies knew that, respected the man, and would have followed him through fire—barefoot—if he'd asked it of them.

Now Custis Long crossed his legs, folded his hands in his lap, and waited for the boss to say what was on his mind.

After a longer than normal pause, Vail said, "I don't know if you're the man for this job, Custis, but you are the one I intend to send. And before you ask, my reluctance is not that I doubt your abilities. I hope you know better than that by now. Rather, this assignment might take some time, and I hate to give you up for that long." •

Longarm's eyebrows shot up, but he kept his mouth shut.

"I received a letter from Jace Bartlett. Do you know him?"

"No, sir. I don't call him to mind," Longarm said.

"Jace is the marshal assigned to the Missouri-Arkansas District."

Longarm grunted. "All right. That's where I heard the name before. Political hack, ain't he."

Billy coughed into his fist. "That is *not* the way we might want to put that, Custis."

"Yes, sir. Sorry." He was not at all sorry, but saying so seemed the right thing to do here.

"Jace is having problems with non-tax-paid whiskey."

"Moonshine," Longarm prompted.

"Non-tax-paid," Billy corrected.

"Yes, sir. Sorry." Longarm reached into his coat pocket and brought out a cheroot. He bit the twist off the end and stuck the slim cigar between his teeth.

"Are you listening, Longarm?"

"Yes, sir. Absolutely."

"What? You're not going to say you're sorry this time?" Billy said sarcastically.

"I hadn't intended to, boss, but I will if you like."

"I . . . forget it. The thing is, I want you to go to Springfield. Contact Jace. See what he wants you to do."

"Yes, sir. Springfield. That would be Missouri? Or Massachusetts?"

"Has anyone ever mentioned, Custis, that you can be a smart-ass?"

"Oh, yes, sir. Many times."

"Well, I can certainly believe that." Billy sighed.

Heavily. Then he said, "See Henry on your way out. He has travel vouchers and whatnot for you."

"Yes, sir. May I ask something, sir?"

"Go ahead."

"Can I leave in the morning? I, uh, I have a bit of an engagement this evening."

"I suppose so, considering how late you were getting back from lunch. Same lady?"

Longarm grinned. "No, sir. Different one tonight."

"Lord, I am glad I'm no longer a bachelor. All that would kill me at my age."

"Yes, sir, it likely would," Longarm said, still grinning.

"Longarm!"

Longarm turned and got the hell out of there before Billy heaved something at him.

Chapter 2

The hansom cab pulled to a stop outside the hotel. Long-arm dismounted first then helped Elizabeth to the sidewalk. He looked up at the cabbie, perched high in the driving box, and said, "Wait here. I won't be but a few minutes."

"Yes, sir."

Longarm handed the man a silver dollar to make sure he would be there when Longarm came back out, then he offered his arm to Elizabeth and squired her inside.

She collected her room key, and he walked with her to the foot of the stairs.

"Will you come up?" she asked.

Longarm gave her a gentle smile and said, "I think not. It has been a lovely evening, but our first. The first of many, I hope. Perhaps the next time your troupe plays Denver." He took her hand, bowed over it, and kissed the air a fraction of an inch above the back of her hand.

"Goodness, I . . . Thank you, Custis. It was lovely."

"Sleep well, dear. Good night now." He turned and headed back out to the cab, quite pleased with himself.

Playing the gentleman had its advantages, he had found.

For one thing it confused a lady to have a man voluntarily do without a wrestling match. And confusing a woman was always a good idea.

Moreover, it would intrigue her. And perhaps worry her. Was there something wrong with her appearance? Did she have a body odor that turned the gentleman away?

Longarm would let her stew on that tonight. And the next time she hit Denver, he would be certain to have her for the night.

As for now . . .

He went back out to the waiting cab and gave the driver another address.

By his calculations, Jessica should be finishing her last performance just about now. If he hurried, he would get to the backstage door at approximately the same time that she was refreshed, dressed, and ready for an evening on the town.

As for himself, Longarm figured he could sleep on the train.

He leaned out the window and called up to the cabbie, "Hurry, please, driver."

Chapter 3

The hansom rocked to a stop in front of a small house close in to Denver's business district. Longarm climbed down from the coach, and the driver called out, "Do I wait, sir?"

Longarm grinned up at the man with the top hat and whip and said, "Not this time, friend." He handed the driver another dollar and bade him a good night.

While the cab clip-clopped away into the night, Longarm walked up the narrow flagstone path to the front porch. As soon as his footsteps sounded on the boards, the door was flung open and a young woman motioned for him to come inside.

When he did so, she threw herself into his arms and did her level best to lick his tonsils.

"Yeah," he said when the two of them came up for air, "but are y' glad to see me."

Laughing, she took him by the arm and led him into the parlor. "One drink," she said, "two at the most, then it's up to bed we go."

"What's this?" Longarm demanded. "D'you have designs on my body, madam?"

"Sir, I not only have designs on you, I intend to fuck you into the ground."

Longarm kissed her again, then took a step backward so he could look at her. And nice she was to look at, too.

Janeth Peterson was perhaps in her upper twenties or early thirties—he had never asked—tall, slim, with hair the color of honey. She had sparkling brown eyes, lush full lips, and a healthy swell of breast. She was wearing a silk robe . . . and nothing underneath it, as was delightfully evident.

Longarm reached forward and plucked the bow that tied her robe closed. Once free of that constraint, the robe fell partially open, displaying Janeth's body. And dark vee of pubic hair below a soft, pale bulge of belly.

"Forget the drinks," Longarm said. "I can get that anyplace."

She came into his arms again and reached up to kiss him. Then dropping her arms, she shrugged the robe off her shoulders. The silken material slithered to the floor. Longarm picked her up and carried her to the sofa. He sat, keeping Janeth in his arms, and most thoroughly kissed the lady.

"I want you," she whispered. "I've been waiting all evening to see you." She giggled. "I blew my lines twice during the second act. I was thinking about you instead of what I was doing up there."

"Aye, an' now I'm here, ready t' play," he said, smiling, running his hands over her body, caressing and teasing and pleasing her. He fingered her pussy, and she quickly reacted with a shuddering climax that left her breathless and flushed.

Janeth recovered her breath and shivered, then slid off his lap to kneel on the floor at his feet. She unbuttoned Longarm's trousers and reached inside to take hold of his cock and bring it out where she could see it. And taste it.

Peeling his foreskin back, she ran her tongue around

and around the red, engorged bulb of the head of his massive dick, then up and down the length of it.

"So pretty," she murmured, taking it into her mouth. She pulled away for a moment to ask, "Do you want to cum in my mouth, Custis?"

"Want to, yes. Going to, no. I want your body the first time." He smiled. "After that we'll just have t' see what happens."

Janeth stood and took his hand. She pulled him off the couch and led him up a flight of stairs to her bedroom and to the big canopy bed. She helped pull his clothes off and, when he was naked, drew him down onto the feather mattress beside her.

Longarm fondled the girl, kissing and touching her, holding her close.

He pulled her legs apart and lay on top of her. Janeth guided his cock into the hot, wet depths of her pussy. Her flesh surrounded him as he sank into her, filled her. Pleased her.

Slowly he began to stroke in and out. Janeth responded, her hips moving in rhythm with his strokes. Quicker. Harder. Deeper. Until he was plunging himself in and out, their bellies slapping together, their breathing rapid.

Janeth cried out as she reached her climax moments before Longarm came, his jism spurting deep into her body.

She wrapped her arms and legs tightly around him and held him there for long minutes, keeping him from withdrawing until both of them became calm again.

"Nice," she whispered.

Longarm grinned. "For openers. Now let's see what else we can do here." And once again he began to stroke slowly in and out, Janeth's hips responding.

Chapter 4

There were two ways to get to Missouri. One would be to take the Denver & Rio Grande south to Pueblo, then the Santa Fe east into Missouri, and a stagecoach south to finish off the trip. The other would be to take the Union Pacific east to Omaha and a paddlewheeler south to Saint Louis and finally a stagecoach back west again to reach Springfield.

Longarm, not surprisingly, chose to head for Omaha and the plush pleasures of the 140-foot sidewheeler, the *Boudica*.

His badge was all he needed for passage on the railroad, but he had to spend one of the travel vouchers Henry had given him in order to get his ticket on the first boat moving south. That happened to be the *Boudica*, captained by Master Seaman James Harrison and populated with some of the best-looking casino shills Longarm had seen in a long time.

As soon as he had his carpetbag aboard, he headed for the lounge. And the array of gaming tables, each attended by a stunningly beautiful woman in an evening gown and tiara.

It seemed a little early in the day for such finery, but

what did he know about the boat or her requirements? All he really cared about was that the passengers need not be in formal attire.

He played a little chuck-a-luck, long enough to decide that he would not be making any fortunes that way, then drifted over to one of the poker tables. He spent the rest of the day there, enjoying the low-stakes play and the quality of the rye whiskey the *Boudica* stocked.

Late in the afternoon he gathered his money and pushed back from the table.

"Thank you, gentlemen," he said with a tip of his Stetson. "It's been pleasant, but hunger calls."

"Come back after you've et," one of the players invited. "We'll be here."

Longarm did not see the young woman who had been waiting on him during the afternoon so he ambled across the casino floor to the bar built in between two staircases leading to staterooms on the upper deck. He wanted to tip the waitress and the bartender.

When he was half a dozen steps from the bar, he heard a voice rising loud and shrill. "You black son of a bitch! Don't you backtalk me. Don't you never talk that way to a white man."

The voice was followed by the sound of a hard slap and a whimper.

A man wearing a silk shirt with ruffled cuffs was the complaining party. An elderly Negro stood behind the bar, his expression calm, his eyes down, avoiding looking at the passenger who had just slapped him.

"Nigger," the passenger snarled.

Longarm took the few steps to the bar. He was smiling but there was no mirth in the expression. "Whoa up there, neighbor. There's no need t' get all het up here. Calm down an' leave be, why don't you?"

"Why don't you mind your own fucking business," the passenger barked.

Longarm's smile just got bigger. "'Cause I don't damn well feel like it," he said. "You've just gone an' hit my father. Now surely you don't think I oughta let go o' that without offering a word o' advice to you."

"When I want your advice, I'll ask for it. And don't tell me this man is your papa. Shit, man, you're white as I am."

"Well, you see, he's *like* a father to me," Longarm explained, still smiling. "An' besides, if you don't apologize to the gentleman right this minute, I am gonna beat you within a inch o' your useless life."

The smile remained fixed firmly in place throughout.

"You wouldn't—"

"In a heartbeat," Longarm said.

"Fuck you, mister."

Longarm stepped forward, took hold of the man's hand. Except he took it in the standard police grip that squeezed the bones of the hand in such a way as to cause excruciating pain.

The passenger went to his knees, his face suddenly drained of all color by the agony he was experiencing. "All right. All right. I give."

"Fine," Longarm said. "Now apologize."

"Fuck you."

"That's a mighty thin apology. 'Bout ten more seconds an' I break some bones." Longarm was no longer smiling.

"You can't be seri— Ow, oh, Jesus. All right, mister. Let up, will you!"

"Be glad to. Soon as you apologize," Longarm said calmly.

"I . . . shit. I'm, uh, sorry."

"Louder."

"I said I'm sorry."

"Say it again. But real loud this time. I want to hear that you mean it."

"All right, damnit, I'm sorry, really and truly sorry."

"Now see, that wasn't all that difficult, was it?" Longarm

let go of the man's hand. The fellow snatched it to his chest and cradled it there.

Ignoring the asshole, Longarm stepped forward to the bar. He dropped a silver peso, as good as a dollar anywhere, into the tip jar and skidded another just like it across the bar to the black bartender. "Here you go," Longarm said, raising a finger to the brim of his Stetson.

The old man nodded and mumbled something Longarm could not hear. No matter, he thought.

He was hungry and his thoughts quickly turned to the dining room and what he might find there. He paid no further attention to the unhappy passenger.

Chapter 5

Dining room? Or salon? Longarm wondered which it was called. He was not very adept with nautical terminology. Not that it made any difference. Whatever one chose to call it, the dining room was every bit as elegant as the casino. It was awash in white linen and teardrop crystal, and liveried waiters attended to every whim.

Most important to his mind was that the food was extraordinary. He had baked passenger pigeon, a potato puff, steamed asparagus, and the best coffee he could ever remember tasting.

When he walked out to take a turn around the deck, he was overfull. But happy.

The chug and hiss of the engine, the slap and splash of the paddles, and the soft sounds of moving water lulled his senses. The rushing river showed pinpoints of light reflected from the brilliant stars wheeling overhead.

All in all it was about as pleasant and relaxing an evening as he'd ever had . . . well, almost as relaxing. It would have taken first place if he'd had a little female companionship.

He briefly considered approaching one of the beauties who worked the casino. Except he had spent part of the evening watching—and silently laughing at—the passengers who foundered on the rocks of those lovely ladies. Gentleman after gentleman took his best shot at luring one of the women. And woman after woman shot the poor suckers down.

Longarm did not particularly want to join the ranks of that club. It seemed best just to enjoy the fresh air on deck, smoke a final cigar, and head for his stateroom. Alone.

The *Boudica* did have a fine-looking collection of dealers, though. Longarm was smiling at the thought of them as he reached the foredeck and walked out beside the heavy cargo boom. He leaned on the rail and fished a cheroot out of his pocket, bit the twist off, and spat it out then reached into his vest pocket for a lucifer.

Longarm turned to put the breeze at his back so he could light the match. That simple act may well have saved his life.

He saw a flash in a shadow on the upper deck overlooking the foredeck.

Saw a flare of bright light and heard the snap of a small-caliber bullet sizzling past his head.

Saw a dark figure detach itself from the shadows and race aft along the promenade that ran around the upper deck.

Longarm's .45 was instantly in his hand, but quick as he was, the shadowy figure was out of sight even quicker.

Some son of a bitch had just tried to kill him.

And he did not know who or why.

Longarm shoved his Colt back into its leather and ran into the casino, where those twin staircases led upward, up to where the shooter had been.

Chapter 6

The upper deck had at least a dozen people standing, walking, talking. He had no idea which of them, if any, the shooter might have been. It was entirely possible that the bastard had disappeared into a stateroom.

Longarm disliked the idea of allowing someone to remain free after shooting at him, but he had little choice in the matter. He did circulate around the deck, making the full circuit four times, but he could not spot anyone he thought might have taken that shot.

Finally he approached a white-haired gentleman whose clothing suggested he was a Southern planter and asked, "Par'n me, sir, but have you seen anyone running past? Maybe with a pistol in his hand?"

"No, son. I heard a shot from the other side of the boat." The old fellow smiled. "I hope you will understand if I admit that I did not go investigate. I was shot at quite enough a few years back and don't relish the thought of inviting any more of it."

"The War Between the States?" Longarm asked.

"You mean the War for Southern Independence?" the

old gentleman countered. "No, I saw enough action in the Mexican War to satisfy any cravings I might have had. Are you the party who was shot at?"

"I was, sir," Longarm said.

"But you suffered no harm," his companion said.

"No, sir."

The old planter smiled again. "Perhaps you would join me in my cabin. I have some excellent sipping whiskey that would be just the thing to settle the nerves. I would enjoy the pleasure of your company. I know no one aboard and do dearly love to ramble. May I tempt you?"

"Tempt and satisfy alike," Longarm said. "Lead the way, sir. I'll be happy to follow."

"Then perhaps I should introduce myself, sir. I am Charles Leon Smoak, late of Saint Tammany Parish, a pauper now thanks to the damnyankees. But unbowed, sir. Unbowed."

Smoak extended his hand, and Longarm was pleased to shake it. He introduced himself but by name only. He did not admit to the old gentleman that he was an employee of the same damnyankee government that had destroyed whatever holdings Smoak might once have had.

He followed the gentleman to his cabin—it was even smaller than Longarm's stateroom—and spent a most enjoyable evening listening to the old fellow ramble.

And the sipping whiskey was indeed excellent. Illegal whiskey. But excellent. Longarm was careful to refrain from asking where the liquor had come from lest he have to do something about enforcing federal laws against making it.

Inwardly he sighed. Whoever made this smooth, soft whiskey was a master craftsman. Longarm hoped this Missouri assignment was not going to involve that particular gentleman. The crime, in his opinion, would be to put the man out of business, tax-paid or non-tax-paid.

Chapter 7

When Longarm's yawns outnumbered his answers, he excused himself and thanked Smoak for the pleasure—and a genuine pleasure it had been, too—of his company. He went back onto the stateroom deck and paused there to remember where his room was. He had barely seen it when he came aboard and now had to think back in order to remember which it was.

His good intentions about sleeping on the train east had all been for naught. There had been a group of friendly fellows with a deck of cards, and that had been that. Longarm came off the train in Omaha twelve dollars richer than when he boarded the U.P. coach.

But now he was tired. He wanted nothing more than to crawl into his bunk and sleep until they reached Cape Girardeau, which the ticket agent has assured him was closer to Springfield than Saint Louis would have been.

Then, damnit, he might sleep on the stagecoach, too.

Yawning, he started walking aft, footfalls ringing hollow on the decking, and noticed a movement in the shadows halfway along the promenade.

Something about the furtive motions caught Longarm's eye. And raised red flags in his consciousness. Despite how weary he was after all that travel, he became instantly alert to the possible danger.

He watched the dark figure standing ahead of him on the narrow promenade.

There was something . . .

Longarm flattened himself against a doorway to one of the staterooms and pulled his .45 seconds ahead of another snap and flash from the hand of the unknown person in the shadows.

His Colt thundered, the sound of it completely overpowering that of the small-caliber revolver at the far end of the deck.

Longarm heard the dull, meaty thud of lead striking flesh, and a man's form detached itself from the shadows.

He stepped out in plain sight, so Longarm shot the son of a bitch again.

The man grunted, spun halfway around to his left, and fell over the railing onto the churning sidewheel paddles.

Within seconds he was gone, driven underneath the dark waters of the Missouri by the turning wheel, silvery in the moonlight.

Longarm still had no idea who he had shot—or whether it was his bullet or the river that killed him—until the next morning when the purser, a man named Benning, approached him to ask if he had seen his adversary from the previous evening.

"I'm not sure who you mean by that," Longarm responded.

"The man you threatened to beat after he slapped our bartender. His friends say they haven't seen him since last night, and they have searched all over the boat."

"No," Longarm said, "I don't know where he might've got to." Which was not exactly a lie. Longarm did not know exactly where the body was now.

Chapter 8

Cape Girardeau was not the sleepy little town Longarm expected. Rather, it was raw and brash and very busy. The *Boudica* was the third boat tied up at the docks, the others loading—or unloading, he did not pause to find out which—cargo.

Longarm was one of two passengers to disembark. He walked west from the levee, past the dives where sailors and stevedores drank, to a quieter, gentler part of town.

The barman in a pleasant saloon with a billiard table but no whores told Longarm where he could find the stagecoach depot. The gent also served up beer that was cold and crisp and foamy, something that had not been possible on the *Boudica*, something to do with storage afloat. He also had a more than decent assortment of cigars to offer, including a cheroot that was fresh and flavorful.

Longarm rather wished he could spend more time with that worthy gentleman, instead bowing to duty and lugging his carpetbag to the stage depot.

"Sure thing, Marshal. We have a coach leaving this

evening. Seven p.m. sharp. Will you be wanting a space on it?" the friendly clerk said.

"I will," Longarm confirmed. "Seven o'clock, you say? That gives me time to have a bite o' supper beforehand."

"Can I recommend a place then? Good cooking, clean, I think you would like it. Most everybody does."

The restaurant was every bit as good as the stage clerk suggested. Longarm treated himself—or rather, the tax-payers treated him—to a thick steak with all the trim-mings and he topped the meal off with a slab of rhubarb pie that was tart and sweet and to die for.

He felt good when he walked out of Cara's Fine Dining.

He felt considerably less good the next afternoon when he located U.S. Marshal Jason Bartlett's office and reported for duty there.

"Where the hell have you been?" the marshal de-manded, raising his voice and wagging an accusatory fin-ger in Longarm's face. "You should have been here days ago. Let me make this clear, Long. I won't put up with slackness in this office. Your man Vail might, but get that through your head. As long as you are in this office, you will abide by my rules. And foremost among those rules is promptness. Do I make myself clear, Long?"

Fortunately the man did not pause in his tirade long enough for Longarm to answer that question. He might have been very unhappy with any comment Longarm might have made.

But Jace Bartlett did indeed make himself clear.

Chapter 9

"You're Long?" The man asking the question was a lean, aging fellow with gray liberally sprinkled through his hair. He wore a Colt and looked like he knew how to use it.

"I am," Longarm acknowledged.

The man stuck his hand out to shake. "I'm Mark Loomis. I'm his chief deputy. Welcome. Care to go have a drink and get acquainted?"

Longarm nodded. Once they were out of the office and settled at a table in a nearby saloon, he said, "How the hell d'you stand it, Mark?" He did not specify what he meant by that. And did not need to.

"You don't get used to it," Loomis said, "but you do learn to ignore most of what the man says or does. At least if you want to keep your badge, you do."

"I wouldn't think it would always be easy," Longarm said, standing. "Let me buy the first round. What will you have?"

"Beer and a shot. Sit down. They know what I want. Jenny will bring it and take your order." Loomis smiled. "But you can pay if you like."

"Ah, that's nice o' you," Longarm said, beginning to like the chief deputy.

True to the prediction, a young woman—a rather attractive young woman—came to their table, took their orders, and returned with two beers and two shots of whiskey.

When she had gone, Loomis said, "Jenny is a widow. Her husband was one of our deputies. His murder is one of the reasons we're shorthanded now."

"One?" Longarm said. "What are the others?"

"You've already met the other reason. Men hire on, stay a few weeks, and move along. Jace grates on pretty much everybody's nerves, but just about every politician in this end of the state owes him favors. That's why he got the job.

"Mostly Jace plays politics and ignores the workings of the office. I take care of most of that. So in a way you'll be working more for me than for him," Loomis said.

"That's a relief," Longarm said, taking a swallow of his beer. "Say, this is good."

"Brewed up in Saint Louis," Loomis said. "We like it. Anyway, about the job. I suppose they already told you we have a problem with illegal whiskey. There's a lot of it made in the hills down this way, and aside from the loss of taxes, some of it is being made by people who just want the money it can bring and never mind if drinking the shit kills people."

Longarm raised an eyebrow.

"Some of these boys are cutting corners. Using iron pots instead of copper. They quick cook with sugar instead of running the product through twice. Are you familiar with whiskey making?"

"A little," Longarm said, "but no more than that."

"Tomorrow I'll take you out to a still and show you the process."

Again Longarm's eyebrow went high.

"Don't worry. It isn't in operation these days, but I keep it intact so I can use it to show new fellows what it's all about." He smiled. "The man who was operating it did six months and is on probation now. One of the conditions of his probation is that he guards that still and gives his talks on its operation. Nice man. Which you will find is pretty normal around here. Most of these small operators are just family men who are trying to make a little extra above what they can produce on their farms. They don't think of themselves as criminals although they know they can go to jail if they get caught."

"It sounds as if you like them," Longarm said.

"I do. Most of them anyway. But here lately, there are some in the game just for money. Big money. They don't care about quality, and if someone goes blind . . . or even dies . . . from drinking their product, that's their own look-out, the way these bastards think. It's those operators that I'm hoping you can help bring down."

Longarm nodded and took another drink. The whiskey was decent, the beer exceptional.

"Drink up, Long. We need to go find you a place to stay while you're here, and you will need a horse and such." Loomis smiled. "You'll be going places where there's no public transportation, that's for sure."

Longarm finished his drinks and stood. "Ready when you are, Mark."

Chapter 10

The room Mark took him to was not as large, nor as comfortable, as his room back home in Denver, but with any kind of luck, he would not be staying long. It was on the second floor in back so it should be quiet. He hoped.

"No drinking in my rooms and no women," the old harridan who owned the house growled. "The door is locked at ten p.m. sharp, no exceptions. And I don't serve meals. This is a rooming house, not a boardinghouse, so mind the difference. I don't do laundry either. There's a Chinese laundry two blocks over and one down. Mr. Loomis can show you where. I do change the sheets, once a week on Saturdays. I expect you to clean yourselves before you get in bed and dirty the clean sheets, but that's up to you. One towel each Saturday as well. Carry your own water up, but there is always hot water on the stove downstairs."

Longarm was fascinated by the way a wart on her chin bounced and jiggled when she spoke. Delightful woman, Mrs. Canfield. Salt of the earth. You bet.

She finally ran out of instructions and left Longarm alone to settle in. That did not take long. He unpacked his carpetbag, laid out soap and towel beside the basin . . . and that was that.

It was nigh onto dinnertime, so he went back downstairs and out onto the porch. He did not particularly want another encounter with Mrs. Canfield so he did not ask for her opinions, of which she probably had legion. Besides, he wanted to become at least a little familiar with the neighborhood.

He wandered down the street and into the first café he came to. It was run by a German couple. If the old woman had any English, she was shy about showing the fact, but her husband could make do fairly well.

"Beef," Longarm ordered. "Potatoes. Biscuits."

"Ja, ja." The man hurried away and spoke to his woman, and directly Longarm was served a slab of roast beef that smelled of vinegar and tasted of heaven. It was accompanied not by potatoes but by a noodle dish swimming in spicy gravy. And their coffee was damned good, too.

If these people served breakfast, too, then he needn't look any further for where he would be taking his meals while he was in Springfield.

After dinner he walked off some of the fullness in his belly, not looking for anything in particular, just looking in general.

He sampled the wares in three nearby saloons and decided the best, not surprisingly, was the place where Mark Loomis had taken him earlier. That, too, would serve nicely as his everyday watering hole while he was in town.

He wrapped up his first day as Jason Bartlett's deputy and went back to Mrs. Canfield's rooming house. Before ten o'clock, thank you very much. And up to bed on clean sheets and a very comfortable mattress.

Chapter 11

"I expect results, Long. Results. And be damned quick about it. After all, you'll be dealing with a bunch of country bumpkins. Vail claims you are his best deputy."

Longarm suppressed a smile. Billy's "best" deputy? How about that. It was an opinion Longarm had long held himself. But for Billy to say it? Now that was mighty nice.

"So I want results, Long. Results."

Longarm did not pay much attention to the rest of Jace Bartlett's harangue. Or pep talk. Or whatever the hell it was supposed to be. If the man had any balls, he would be out there leading his people and flushing out the illegal stills. Instead Bartlett stayed safely ensconced behind his desk, no doubt feeling important and above the sweaty deputies who were charged to go out and do his bidding.

Asshole!

"Yes, sir." Longarm threw one of those in every now and then to show that he was paying attention. "It's exactly like you say, sir." Longarm's experience was that assholes like Jason Bartlett liked to be agreed with, and no harm done. But it was all Longarm could do to keep from yawning in the man's face.

Fifteen minutes later when they left Bartlett's office, Mark Loomis motioned for Longarm to follow and walked down the block to a café.

"Two coffees, Martha," he said as they walked in.

Martha was probably as old as Longarm and Loomis together, but she had a great smile and a willing attitude. Longarm liked her. Obviously the chief deputy did, too.

"Did you get all of what the boss was saying?" Loomis asked with a grin.

"No. I was waitin' for him t' say 'good morning' but I never heard those words outa him," Longarm said.

Loomis grunted. "And you probably won't. Jace tends to think of himself as a commander, certainly not as a leader. I suspect you understand the difference."

"Aye, so I do," Longarm said. "So how much o' that shit . . . oh, sorry, ma'am, I shouldn't of said that . . . how much of that stuff am I supposed t' pay attention to?"

"None of it," Loomis said, dragging his coffee mug close and lacing the dark brew with cream and honey. Longarm took his black.

"What I think you should do is to first hire that horse we talked about. Pick one you like and keep him. The office will pay for his hire. I've already talked to Shorty Wright over at the livery. He will see you get something good and steady, for you might be covering any sort of ground on him.

"Then take a few days to wander the hills. Make a wide circle. Don't be in any hurry about it. I want you to have some idea of the country you'll be covering.

"The moonshiners won't have seen you before, and I see no reason why you should announce yourself as a deputy. I see you aren't wearing your badge where it shows. That's good. Keep it that way. You can say . . . oh, you can say whatever you like. Better yet, don't say anything about who you are or what you are doing. If someone wants to think you're on the dodge, so much the better. It might help some of the folks to open up to you."

Loomis laughed. "But don't expect people to start spilling their guts to you just because they think you might be an outlaw. Folks around here are good people. They're friendly. But just on the surface. They won't open up until they have a reason to."

Longarm nodded and tried his coffee. It was hot and pleasant.

"Have you had breakfast?" Loomis asked.

"Ayuh. Before I came in this mornin'," Longarm said.

"Well, I didn't, so set and let me eat a bite." He swiveled around in his chair and waved to get Martha's attention. "I could use some ham and eggs over here," he called.

"And I could use two extra hands, so hold your horses, sonny. I'll get to you in a minute."

Longarm smiled. Yep. He did like Martha. Feisty old bat.

Chapter 12

Shorty Wright was well named. Longarm doubted the man would measure much more than five feet tall. And that was if he was wearing boots.

The man kept good horses, though. Longarm suspected he would have been happy with any of them, especially after some of the army remount animals he had had to put up with over the years.

All of the animals Longarm saw in Shorty's stable were sleek and well muscled, and when approached, they were curious and not especially timid.

"You know your stock, so I'd 'preciate it if you was to advise me about what animal t' take," Longarm said. "Pick out a good 'un for me, if you please."

"I already have," Shorty said. "He's nice mannered and sturdy. Not the fastest I got but probably the steadiest. Smart little son of a bitch, too. Not as smart as a mule, of course, but you won't find any horse that is. He's in this stall back here."

The horse Shorty indicated was 14.3 or 15 hands, wide in the front end, with a nicely shaped head, small muzzle, and large, clear eyes. It was a blood bay with black points and white socks on both hind legs.

Longarm walked around the horse, trailing a hand across its hide as he passed. He was pleased to see that the horse remained calm and relaxed. It had no fear of mankind. When he went to tack it up, it took the bit without balking and did not try to blow its belly when he pulled the cinch tight.

"Satisfied?" Shorty asked when Longarm stepped onto the stock saddle that went with the bay.

"Satisfied," Longarm affirmed. He lightly touched a heel to the bay's flank, and it stepped out at a swift walk.

He found that it was easy to handle, taking its cues from rein or weight shift alike. It had a pleasant enough trot, one that would not rattle a man's teeth, and a delightfully smooth canter.

"Satisfied," Longarm said again when he returned to the barn and led the bay into its stall. "Marshal Loomis has made arrangements for my use of the horse?"

"He has. He said you'll want to keep it here and that I should go right on feeding and grooming. Is that right by you?"

Longarm nodded. "Perfect."

"Come take him out any time of day," Shorty said. "You know where the saddle is. You don't have to tell me. Just act like he belongs to you. Which in a manner of speaking he does, at least for the time being."

"Good enough," Longarm said. "I won't be wanting him today, but I expect to do some riding come morning."

"Then I'll likely see you tomorrow." Shorty turned and went into the office.

Longarm headed for the state capitol building. He wanted to look at some maps of the vicinity if any were available.

Chapter 13

Loomis found Longarm awash in a sea of paper, sitting in a back room with maps spread across the walnut surface of a long table. Longarm looked up at the chief deputy's entry. "How'd you know where t' find me?" he asked.

The deputy chuckled. "We may be the state capital, but fact of the matter is that Springfield is a small town, especially now with the legislature not in session. A stranger stands out."

"I'll have t' keep that in mind," Longarm said.

"The reason I dropped by is to invite you for a drink. I'm going for one and thought you might like to come along," Loomis said.

"I will admit that this is dry and dusty work. A little something to clear the throat wouldn't hurt." Longarm smiled and stood, yawning and stretching. "What time is it anyway?"

"Quitting time," Loomis answered.

"That works for me," Longarm said. "Be all right if I leave these maps here until tomorrow?"

"I would think so."

"Then let's go. Same place as yesterday?" Longarm asked.

The chief deputy nodded. "I'm partial to it."

The two walked over to Loomis's favorite saloon. The young woman—Longarm remembered that her name was Jenny, the widow of a deputy marshal—brought beers and shots without being asked. Loomis paid.

Longarm took a long drink from his beer and said, "That goes down good."

"Did Shorty do right by you?" Loomis asked over the rim of his whiskey glass.

Longarm nodded. "He did. The man keeps fine stock."

"Is there anything else you need?" Loomis asked.

"Nothing I can think of at the moment. Tomorrow I'll try out that horse, get a look around. I may be gone for a few days making that circle you mentioned. After that"—he shrugged—"after that, we'll just have t' see."

"We'll worry about that when the time comes," Loomis said. "But for now"—he smiled—"drink up."

The chief deputy took his own advice and hoisted his mug.

Half an hour later Loomis stood and said, "I have a wife at home who'll soon be after my head if I let supper get cold. You don't have to report to him in the morning. Just go on and do what you need to."

Longarm nodded. "Good enough. I think I'll have one more, then go to supper m'self."

Loomis left and Longarm leaned back and stretched his legs under the table. He lit a cheroot and, when he caught Jenny's eye, raised a finger to indicate he was ready for another.

The girl took a little longer than usual, but when she brought his beer and shot, she also delivered a folded note, then hurried back to the bar.

The note gave an address and the time of 9 p.m.

Longarm carefully folded the piece of paper and slipped it into his pocket. He could not think of any reason why the barmaid would want to lay any sort of trap. Surely she had nothing against him, no reason to dislike him.

The few times he had been into the saloon, he had treated her decently. After all, her late husband had been a deputy also. She surely had nothing against the badge or those who wore it.

She did not look in his direction again while he finished his drinks and left.

Chapter 14

Longarm mulled it over while he was at supper. He knew practically no one in Springfield, and none of them had reason to be mad at him, at least not as far as he knew. He could think of no reason why he should be wary of Jenny's invitation. He decided to show up and see what happened. But to be ready for trouble just in case.

While there was still daylight in the sky, he made a few inquiries—the boy who delivered groceries for Jontiel's Market was the one who set him straight—so he would know where he was going.

The house was one story, shotgun style, built on a narrow city lot. The clapboard siding was in need of paint, and the remnants of a long-ago garden were visible in the tiny patch of earth that passed as a front yard. A picket fence, too, was in need of paint. The gate stood open, one of its hinges broken and sagging.

A shutter had fallen off and was lying propped against the wall.

The place was in need of the little things that a man did to keep his home in order.

Promptly at nine, Jenny opened the door to his tug of the bellpull.

Longarm immediately snatched his hat off.

Since he saw her in the saloon, she had changed clothes. Done something to her hair. Seemed . . . fresh now. And even prettier than she did when at work.

Jenny was five foot five or six, slim, with hair the color of wild honey. He guessed she was in her early to mid-thirties. She was wearing a plum-colored silk dressing gown that clung nicely to her figure, and her hair was loose and flowing, falling down to the middle of her back where before it had been pinned up.

At work she presented herself as fairly drab. Deliberately, no doubt, to avoid unwanted advances from the customers. He understood that. Now . . . she was exceptionally pretty. Her cheeks had color. A touch of rouge? Perhaps. He was not sure. It could also have been that she was flushed with excitement for some reason or because she had been hurrying since she got off work.

He thought he could detect a light scent of flowers. Some perfume or toilet water, no doubt.

He looked at her and suddenly wished he had thought to bring her flowers. She was that kind of woman. She made him want to please her.

"They call you Longarm," she said. "You're from Denver. You aren't married." She smiled. "I asked Mark about you. Please come in."

He did. The house was small, very tidy, dark with the roller shades pulled down. The overstuffed furniture filled the front room to capacity and then some.

Jenny took his hat and hung it on a peg beside the front door.

"Your note . . ."

"I didn't want to be too explicit," she said, a comment that caused Longarm's eyebrow to rise in inquiry. "If anyone else should see that note, it would cause problems for me at work.

Not with my boss. She is very understanding. With the customers, I mean. But I'm being rude. Please sit down."

She indicated an armchair that had a reading lamp beside it, lit now but with the wick turned low, and a foot stool in front of it. Judging from the size and the sagging seat cushion, Longarm guessed this would have been her late husband's chair.

"Can I get you something to drink? Are you hungry?"

Longarm answered no to both questions. Jenny seemed nervous for some reason. But then she was a widow living alone and there was a strange man in her house as the sun was going down. Perhaps she had reason to be nervous, either because of him or the neighbors.

She perched on the footstool immediately in front of him and leaned in close. Her expression was serious.

"You know that I am widowed," she said.

Longarm nodded.

"If I were to give in to any of the advances made by my customers, I would never have a moment's peace afterward. People would talk. Women can be quite vicious, you know. Men, too, for that matter. So I must be chaste and proper, especially so since I work in a saloon. I don't want to be the butt of gossip."

"I can surely understand that," Longarm said.

"But I have . . . needs. Desires. I am a young woman still, and I would like to have a child. Can you understand that, too?"

"I think so," he answered. "I think I can."

"What I am asking, what I invited you here for . . . would you give me a child, Mr. Longarm?"

If he had not already been sitting, he suspected he would have fallen down.

"A . . . child?"

"At least try for one," she said. "Would you do that for me?"

Jenny stood and opened the plum-colored silk gown. She wore nothing underneath it.

Chapter 15

She tasted of cinnamon and . . . something else that he could not identify.

She felt good in his arms. She fit there just fine, as if she belonged. As if he had been waiting just for this pleasure.

Jenny was not shy about her charms. She seemed comfortable without clothes. And she looked damned good naked. Slim and straight with small, pale nipples perched atop firm, perky tits. Not overly large but more than a mouthful.

Her waist was tiny. He had not noticed that when she was dressed, but now he could see how very slight she was. It was not possible, of course, but he almost thought he could circle her waist with his two hands. Yet she had a lovely swell of hip. And a soft, curly patch of fur at her crotch.

He carried her through the kitchen and on into the bedroom at the back of the shotgun house. Longarm lay down beside her, enjoying the feel of her slim body against his.

Jenny toyed with his dick, running the foreskin up and down, feeling it, playing with his balls.

"Nice," she said.

"So are you," Longarm told her. "You're very nice indeed."

He sucked on her tits and slipped a finger inside her. She was already wet and ready for him.

"Do you want me to suck you?" she asked.

"Later." He smiled. "We got time t' try it all."

Jenny sighed and held her arms open to him. And her thighs.

She gasped a little when he filled her. But he did not think she was complaining.

Jenny began very slowly and softly to rotate her hips. "Can you brace yourself and hold still there?" she asked.

"I reckon."

"Try not to move. Let me do it all."

Longarm nodded and did as she asked, holding himself poised on top of her while Jenny very gently fucked him. Back and forth. Up and down. Round and round.

He laughed. "Now I know where the term *screwing* comes from. That's what it feels like."

Jenny seemed to delight in that. She joined him in his laughter. After only a few seconds she stopped.

"Is somethin' wrong?" he asked.

"I just thought . . . I could be wrong, but I think that's the first good laugh I've had since Carl was killed."

"D' you want to talk about it?"

"Later maybe." She smiled. "Not now." She resumed screwing him while he held—or tried to hold—completely still above her.

Surprisingly quickly Longarm felt the gather and rise of his sap until he exploded inside Jenny's body, his juices filling her pussy and oozing out onto his balls.

Unable to hold himself above her any longer, Longarm collapsed onto the girl's body. After a few seconds he asked, "Am I too heavy on you?"

Jenny tightened her arms around him and shook her

head. "I like the feel of you there. Stay for just a bit, will you?"

It was a request he did not mind fulfilling. He might even have dozed a little while he lay on her. Soon though his cock filled and lengthened once again.

Jenny felt the change and was smiling. But this time she let Longarm do the screwing.

Chapter 16

Longarm overslept the next morning. Not actually sleeping but in bed nonetheless.

"I don't have to go to work until ten, so don't even think about getting up early," Jenny warned.

Afterward she let him wash and dress while she fixed breakfast for the two of them. It was very domestic, he thought. And wondered if she did indeed have the baby she had been craving. For her sake, he hoped that she did.

On the other hand, a child would certainly compromise her standing in the community. Still, Jenny seemed like a strong-willed young woman. He was sure she would have considered all the pros and cons of her choice. And it was her choice to make, not his.

"Would you like a late supper tonight?" she offered. And wrinkling her nose, "And something more after?"

Longarm kissed the girl and tapped the tip of her nose. "I'd love to, but I'll be gone for the next couple days. Will that invitation still be open when I get back?"

"Yes. Absolutely." She hesitated. "If you are as good a listener as you are a lay . . . I'd like to talk a little."

"About Carl?" he guessed.

She nodded. "Yes." With a sigh she added, "I loved that man. I really did. It hasn't been easy without him." Longarm thought he saw tears welling up in the corners of her eyes.

For some reason the tears—her vulnerability perhaps—made his dick harden. He wanted her.

When he got back, he thought. Not now. Not while her thoughts were about her dead husband.

"I don't know why you are here," she said, "but be careful. Carl was looking for illegal whiskey stills when he was murdered. They shot him down, Custis. They shot him from ambush and burned his body thinking to cover up the murder."

"Were the killers caught?" Longarm asked.

Jenny shook her head. "No. As far as I know, no one even looked for them." She wrung her hands. "Oh, I shouldn't say that. Mark is a dear man and a fine officer of the law."

"And Bartlett?" he asked.

"Don't get me started on that son of a bitch," she said. "Sorry. That just slipped out. A lady shouldn't talk like that. Which just proves that I'm no lady."

He kissed her. "You are lady enough for me, ma'am." Then he laughed. "We were going to talk when I get back, weren't we."

"Do you mind?" she asked, looking like she was genuinely concerned that she might have bothered him.

"Not at all." He kissed her again. "Any time. An' that's a promise. Now if you'll excuse me, I gotta go earn all that money the government pays me."

Jenny laughed. But then she knew more than most civilians about the limitations imposed by a deputy marshal's pay.

"I'll see you when I get back," he said. "An' that's a promise, too."

Chapter 17

Shorty had the bay horse sleek and pretty as a new calf. The little hostler grabbed the saddle Longarm had chosen and threw it on the bay before Longarm had a chance to act. He would deserve something of a tip when the animal was returned, Longarm thought. But that would be his own, not on the government's nickel.

"I'm gonna take a little pasear around this part o' the country," Longarm said as he stepped into the saddle, "so don't be worryin' if I'm gone for a few days."

Shorty grinned up at him, exposing yellowed and broken teeth. "Won't worry me if you take off complete. If the horse don't come back, the marshal's office will be on the hook for it, not me."

Longarm chuckled and nodded and touched the brim of his Stetson to the little fellow. "G'day, Shorty."

The bay horse was a pure pleasure to ride, as he had ascertained when he chose the animal. It took its gaits and held them without a lot of surplus prompting from rein and spur, and its lope was as smooth as its walk. If Longarm had any use for a horse of his own, he would want to buy this one. But a man who lived in a city had no business owning a saddle horse, especially since his work allowed him to borrow the use of a government mount whenever he needed one.

He started off to the east and was amazed anew at how green and overgrown Missouri could be. A man who became nervous in small spaces would not do well there, especially if he—like Longarm—was accustomed to being able to see pretty much horizon to horizon.

He wondered if Easterners became equally uncomfortable when they came west, where the prairies were broad and the mountains high.

The truth was that Longarm was a little nervous about being hemmed in on all sides like this.

His nervousness quite possibly saved his life.

Chapter 18

Longarm turned in the saddle to look behind, along his backtrail. A moment after he did so, a bullet sizzled past his left shoulder.

He instantly dropped from his saddle, hit the ground with his .45 already in hand, and rolled to the side.

The bay horse sidestepped to keep from stepping on him.

Longarm came to his knees, searching for a target.

All he saw was a wisp of white smoke curling up from a thicket of wild sumac.

A moment after that he heard the sounds of hoofbeats receding. The horse was running hard and fast.

Scowling, Longarm stood and shoved his Colt back into its leather. He brushed the dirt from his clothes and reclaimed the reins of the bay.

His mood could have been better.

Jenny's husband, Carl, had been murdered from ambush while he was investigating the illegal whiskey makers.

And now it seemed someone knew who he was and why he was in Missouri.

Longarm was willing to stand up face-to-face against any son of a bitch. But he loathed and despised the sort of low-life bastard who would backshoot a man and, worse, do it from hiding. He figured there should be an especially painful corner of Hell reserved for that sort.

He walked over to the spot where he had seen the smoke, but there was no sign left by the ambusher. A pile of moist turds showed where the man's horse had been tied, well off the trail and out of sight, but in the thick leaf litter of the forest floor Longarm's tracking skills were not enough to allow him to follow.

Frustrated and more than a little pissed off, Longarm returned to the bay horse and stepped into the saddle.

It occurred to him that the ambusher, whoever he was, had to have been observing him this morning. He had chosen a path more or less at random. Certainly he had not had a particular route in mind when he left the city for his get-acquainted loop through the country he needed to cover.

So it would have been impossible for someone to set an ambush ahead of time.

The whiskey makers, whoever they were, had someone in town to look after their interests.

That, Longarm thought, was but a tiny piece of the puzzle he needed to solve. Tiny. But nonetheless important.

Small though it was, it was a start.

And something he damn sure would not forget.

He heeled the bay into motion once again.

Chapter 19

Thick forests, small farms, shallow clear-running streams, hill and valley, green everywhere the eye landed. This was not the sort of country Longarm was accustomed to, but it had its own brand of beauty and he could appreciate its appeal.

He followed whatever road or trail he happened upon with no particular plan or object, stopped at a farmhouse with the intention of buying a meal, and was welcomed in as if a member of the family. Then afterward the man of the house refused payment.

He spent the first night at a crossroads inn, the second camping beside a thin run of water, and a third sleeping on a mat in the back room of a tiny store. Everywhere he went, he encountered smiles and welcome.

Most of the time Longarm had no idea if he was in Missouri or Arkansas. And no need to care which was which. Both were green and rolling and well watered.

It was the water, he knew, that made the production of whiskey possible. Water for the process and wood for the cooking fires. And grain. Corn or barley or rye, it all could be converted into whiskey.

The small farms he passed all seemed to be growing grain. Grain in bulk was difficult to transport to market; whiskey made from that grain was more efficiently moved.

He liked the people he found. But he wondered where their market was to sell their grain.

He asked no questions. Kept his eyes and ears open.

Nearly everywhere he went, he was offered whiskey to drink. It always was poured from a jug or a jar, never from a proper bottle. He doubted that he could have found a pint of tax-paid whiskey if he searched every house and store he passed, but there was plenty of the other sort.

Some of it, he had to admit, was damned good whiskey. It went down smooth and lay warm and easy in the belly.

Other jugs were raw and fiery.

Always Longarm accepted the hospitality but was careful to avoid giving away anything more than his name. It someone wanted to assume he was on the dodge, that was perfectly all right with him.

He saw no stills although it was likely that he met a good many who were producers of the illegal whiskey. And a good many who were not. The question was how to tell one from the other.

His swing through the countryside was for the most part a joy.

Then on the fourth day, after he pointed the bay back in the direction of Springfield, things changed.

But not for the better.

Chapter 20

"Hold it there, mister."

Longarm reined the bay to a halt. There were two of them blocking the road, trapdoor rifles slanting across bony chests.

"Howdy." He smiled and touched the brim of his Stetson by way of a greeting. "What can I do for you gents?"

"You got something of ourn." The one doing the talking was a tall, lean scarecrow of a man with a week's worth of beard. He turned his head and spat a stream of yellow tobacco juice onto the roadway.

"Funny," Longarm said, "but I don't remember taking hold o' anything belongs to you boys."

Ah, there, he thought. Up on the ridge, half hidden in the trees. A third man. Almost had to be part of this deal.

He smiled and nodded, pretending not to understand what was going on here.

"That horse, mister. Handsome animal. It be ourn."

"Is that a fact? Well, I'll be damned." Longarm shook his head in wonder. "This horse looks just exactly like mine. Even sets like him. Now how would you imagine

I went an' made such a mistake as that. Yes, sir, I will be damned. Say, though, I would take it kindly if you was to tell your brother up on the ridge that he oughta come down from there lest I take things wrong an' blow holes through the both o' you."

Longarm turned the bay sideways to the pair, presenting them with a good view of the Colt .45 he had trained on the belly of the spokesman.

Longarm smiled.

The lanky man with the trapdoor musket went pale.

"You see, mister, no matter where that man gets lead into me, I'll still be able to put you down. Likely the both o' you. So if you want t' go on living, you will do me the favor of calling him off."

"I . . . I . . . Billy, bring Jess down from there. D-Do it now."

The other one, shorter and younger than the speaker, turned and cupped his hands. "Jesse. Git down here. Leroy says you's to do it."

There was an answering yell from the ridge and then some crashing through the brush until the one called Jesse emerged. His rifle was also a long-barreled musket except his was a muzzle-loading model. Likely all three of the weapons were surplus military arms with barrels shot out by overuse. Longarm doubted they would keep their shots within a bushel basket at fifty yards.

"You know, boys, if I had time t' spend with you, I'd teach you some o' the finer points of how t' go about robbing folks. You fellas are getting it all wrong. Seems a shame, don't it, that I don't have time t' school you." Longarm grinned and slid his .45 back into the leather.

"We wasn't going to kill you, mister. Just take that good-looking horse," the spokesman said.

"Now, Leroy, you and me an' your brothers here all know that that's a lie. O' course you was gonna kill me.

You couldn't hardly take my horse an' leave me alive to call the law down on you or t' swear vengeance on you. Now could you. So don't be lyin' to me like that, Leroy, or you will piss me off." Longarm's expression and his tone of voice hardened. "An' you don't want t' do that. Trust me."

"I, uh . . ."

"Hush up, Leroy," Billy said.

The one called Jesse just stood there looking confused. Longarm guessed Jesse was perhaps a little soft in the head, even more so than the first two, but perhaps he was the best shot among them.

"Lay your guns down. That's it. Right there in the road. Where-at do you boys live?"

"Yonder," Billy said, pointing to a narrow path that led north along a small creek.

"You farm a little, cook a little, get along like that?" Longarm suggested. "Maybe one o' these times I'll come back an' visit with you. Like if I need a place t' stay for a day or two. That be all right with you boys?"

"We, um, yeah."

"What's your names anyway? You brothers, I take it?"

Billy spoke for them again. "We's the Richardsons. Leroy, William, and Jesse. And we got another brother, Thomas, back to home. If you come this way again . . ."

"If I need to," Longarm said. He wanted them to work out that he was an outlaw, but he could not come right out and say so. "I'll pay you if I do."

"I . . . we . . ."

"Don't be picking those rifles up until I'm well past," Longarm said, "lest I take it unkindly an' set to shooting folks. Now you boys have yourselves a most pleasant day." He laughed. "Better luck with the next son of a bitch as comes along."

He touched the bay's flanks with his heels and put the horse into a lope, riding straight for the men in the road.

The three of them scattered like quail, and Longarm was beyond the Richardson clan.

He felt a tightening between the shoulder blades but did not look behind him to see what the boys were doing with their rifles back there.

Chapter 21

"Marshal Long. Did you have a good trip?"

Longarm swung down off the bay. "Hello, Shorty. It was mostly quiet."

"Did the boy do all right by you?" Shorty took the reins and began unsaddling.

"He did. He's a fine horse. Thanks for picking him." Longarm unstrapped his gear from behind the cantle. He took a quarter eagle from his pocket and gave it to the hostler.

"Oh, you don't have to do that, sir. The marshal's office is paying me."

"I know that, but this is from me."

"Thank you, sir." Shorty pulled the saddle down and dumped it on the stable floor, removed the bridle, and replaced it with a headstall. He picked up a rag and began rubbing the bay down.

Longarm headed for the hotel. He needed a bath and a shave and a change of clothes. And needed, or anyway wanted, to see Jenny again. For more reasons than the obvious.

That evening, refreshed and smelling considerably

better, too, he had supper at the café down the block from the hotel, then walked over to the saloon where Jenny worked.

Her smiled positively lit up the room when Longarm walked in. He sat at a table, and Jenny hurried over to wait on him.

"I'm glad you're safely back. Did you have a good trip?"

"You look nice tonight," he said.

Jenny blushed. "What can I get you?"

"You're changing the subject," he accused.

"Yes, I am," she said. "Now what can I get you?" She looked around as if checking to see whether the boss was becoming annoyed that she was talking with Longarm while there were other customers who needed to be served, too.

Longarm took the hint and gave his order. "Oh, an' I could use some o' them bar cigars. The real ones, though, not the rum crooks."

"I'll bring your order right out to you."

"When d'you get off work?" he asked.

"Eight thirty," she said.

"Be all right if I walk you home?"

"I would be pleased."

He nodded. "Eight thirty then."

Jenny brought him a beer and a shot and a handful of cigars. Longarm picked up his shot glass of whiskey and leaned back in his chair. The evening, he thought, promised to be a good one.

Chapter 22

Longarm was waiting promptly at eight thirty—actually a few minutes before lest he somehow miss her—and offered his arm to the pretty lady.

He squired her onto the boardwalk and escorted her for all to see.

"Won't people talk?" he asked when they were half a block or so down the street.

Jenny giggled and hugged his arm close. "I certainly hope so. If they think I have a steady beau, especially a handsome deputy like you, they just might leave me alone. And wouldn't that be wonderful. So you see, Longarm, you are doing me a favor just by being here and walking with me."

"Longarm?" he asked. "Where'd you hear that moniker?"

She smiled. "Oh, I asked about you. Don't forget, I do have some friends in the marshal's office. They all remember Deputy Carl Roberts. He was a likable man."

"He must have been if he was worthy of your love. You're a good woman, Jennifer."

"Thank you, sir."

"If you don't mind a question," he said.

"Anything."

"While we are on the subject of Carl, did he happen t' leave any notes or comments 'bout these moonshiners he was after? I happened t' think, while I was making that swing around the country, that he will 've known the area an' the people far better'n I possibly could learn in a short time. If he left anything for me t' go by, I'd appreciate a look at it. Is there any such?"

"He had a desk at home. Just a little bit of a thing stuck away in a corner. I haven't had the heart to look through it since he's been gone. But you would be welcome to see if there's anything that would help you." She smiled. "In the morning, though. Not now. I have plans for this evening, you see."

"Ah," he said, grinning. "If they're the sort o' plans I'm thinkin' of, then I agree with you completely."

"Good. Because, yes, those are exactly the sort of plans I have in mind." She hugged his arm close again and laughed as they walked the rest of the way to her house.

Chapter 23

The front door of Jenny's house was barely closed behind them before she started shedding clothes. By the time they reached her bedroom, she was bare-ass naked. And horny. Her nipples were engorged, standing out tall on top of her tits, and her hands were all over Longarm, unbuttoning and unbuckling and practically ripping his clothes off.

"Ah, but did you miss me?" he asked, laughing as he willingly participated in the chore of getting him naked, too.

"You'll never guess," she said. "Now sit down. I want to do something." She smiled. "I've been looking forward to it."

"All right, but—"

"No time for talking. Sit."

"Yes, ma'am." He sat.

Longarm sat on the edge of Jenny's bed. She knelt on the floor between his knees and gently peeled his foreskin back off the erection that had grown along the way.

"Such a lovely thing," she said.

She ran the fingers of one hand lightly up and down the shaft while the other hand toyed with his balls. After several long moments she leaned forward and took the throbbing, eager head into her mouth.

The warmth inside Jenny's mouth felt wonderfully good. Longarm closed his eyes and let the girl suck him. Then, smiling, he opened his eyes again and enjoyed the sight of a pretty woman with his cock distending her cheeks. A woman is never prettier to a man, he thought, than when she has his dick in her mouth.

And that certainly held true with Jenny now.

Longarm groaned and stroked Jenny's hair. She quickly pulled away from him.

"Something wrong?" he asked.

"I don't want you to cum in my mouth," she said.

"Sorry."

"No, it isn't what you think. I would love the taste of your cum. I would drink it every drop. But if you spend it there, you won't have as much left over to put in my cunt, and don't forget, lover, that I am still hoping you will give me a baby. Now lie back. There is something I want to do."

He did as she asked, and Jenny began licking and sucking his balls. Then she moved even lower and tongued his asshole, too.

Longarm could not stand it any longer. He sat upright and took Jenny by the shoulders, picking her up and depositing her onto the bed.

He moved on top of her, inserting a knee between her legs to force her thighs apart—not that very much in the way of force was necessary—and shoving his cock into Jenny's very wet and slippery pussy.

She cried out as he entered.

Immediately Longarm held himself still. "Did I hurt you?"

"No," she told him. "It just feels so good. So wonderful. I've been looking forward to this, too. Now go on, please. Don't leave me hanging."

He pushed the rest of the way into her, and Jenny wrapped her arms tight around him.

The wet heat of her body surrounded him. Pleased him. Became the focus of all his senses.

Longarm held himself deep inside her body. Jenny urged him deeper, pushing his ass with her heels to pull him all the way inside.

He could feel his balls banging against Jenny's ass when he began the sweetness of long, delightful strokes in and out of her flesh.

Jenny began licking and kissing and sucking whatever skin she could reach with her mouth while Longarm continued to slowly fuck her.

Slowly. And then more quickly. And finally with frantic speed until he was pumping hard, his belly pounding hers, his balls slapping hard against her asshole.

Longarm's sap built inside his balls until he could contain it no more, until it exploded out of his dick and deep inside her body.

Jenny cried out, reaching her climax at almost the same time as his. She grasped him hard with arms and legs alike.

And then she collapsed beneath him, passed out cold with the intensity of her release.

Longarm continued to pump cum into her for several seconds. Then finally he withdrew and rolled to the side, breathing as hard as if he'd been running a race.

He smiled and settled down to wait for the girl to wake up.

Chapter 24

Their dawn lovemaking was slow and soft and gentle, and Jenny climaxed at the same time as Longarm. When they were done, he kissed her and carefully withdrew.

"Don't move. You're all wet and messy and sticky," Jenny said as she slipped out from beneath him. "Let me wash you off."

She left the bed and returned moments later with a basin and pitcher and washcloth. She poured a little water into the basin, dunked the washcloth, and wrung out most of the water, then she took his cock in her mouth before carefully wiping his dick clean, peeling the foreskin back and washing the head, cleaning the shaft, and giving his balls a quick wipe as well.

"That water's cold, you know," he said.

"Yes, but you're tough. You can take it," Jenny said.

"Easy for you t' say. You ain't the one being froze here."

"Quit complaining, tough guy."

"I ain't complaining. Just reporting."

She finished cleaning him, dunked the washcloth again,

and scrubbed her pussy with the wet cloth. "Damn," she grumbled. "This water really is cold."

"I think I mentioned that a'ready," Longarm said.

"Yes, but I didn't believe you when it was your privates being frozen. It's another matter entirely when my pussy is the body part in question."

"Serves you right is what I say," Longarm said with a laugh.

When both of them were adequately cleaned, they got up and dressed. "Breakfast?" Jenny said.

"If you're up to making it, I'll damn sure do my part an' eat it," Longarm told her.

"Come on then. You can sit in the kitchen and keep me company while I cook."

After a hearty breakfast and three cups of stout coffee, Longarm said, "Would it be all right if I go through Carl's desk? He might have left something that will be of help."

"Yes, of course. Let me show you where. But . . . but if you don't mind, I would rather not watch while you . . ."

He thought for a moment she was going to cry. Probably Jenny had done a lot of crying since her husband's death. She was a survivor. She would go on. But there was no doubt that she still missed him.

The dead deputy had been a very fortunate man when it came to his home life, Longarm thought, never mind the hard luck he had experienced on the job.

She led him into the front room, to what looked like a schoolhouse desk placed in a corner of the room, close to the side window.

"I'll go wash the dishes while you do"—she took a deep breath—"while you do what you need to."

Longarm kissed her and gave her backside a push in the direction of the kitchen. When Jenny was gone, he sat on the ladderback chair in front of the little desk and opened the top, which also served as the writing surface.

There was little enough inside, but what he did find might well prove to be helpful.

A small notebook contained a list of names. There was no indication as to what those names meant. With luck they were the names of men in the vicinity who were making non-tax-paid whiskey. Or . . . not. There was no explanation, just the names. The Richardson brothers, he noticed, were on the list, but he still did not know why.

Of course, Deputy Carl Roberts would have known what the names meant. Now it would be up to Longarm to find out if he could.

He tore that sheet of paper out of the notebook, folded it, and slipped it into his pocket.

Then he went to find Jenny and ease her feelings with more kisses.

Chapter 25

"You lazy son of a bitch!" Marshal Jason Bartlett screamed.

"Par'n me? Who the hell 're you talkin' about?" Longarm asked, genuinely confused. He had just walked into the office after making his wide, get-acquainted loop through the territory, and now Bartlett was yelling.

"You, damn you," Bartlett yelled with very slightly less volume. "Where have you been?" The question must have been rhetorical because the marshal went on without pause. "I should have known better. I should never have asked for help. I should have known that bastard Vail would send his worst fuckup just to get you out of the office."

Longarm held his tongue somehow—it damn sure was not easy—and looked around for Mark Loomis. The chief deputy was not in at the moment. Not that Longarm blamed him. And if Bartlett had a clerk, that gentleman was absent as well.

"I ought to fire your useless ass," Bartlett complained, his voice rising again in both pitch and volume. "I ought to send you right back to that prick Vail, that's what I ought to do."

That was just about all Longarm could stand listening to. It was one thing to call him names, quite another when the idiot insulted Billy Vail.

"Listen to me, you useless little pencil pusher," Longarm snarled. "United States Marshal William Vail is ten times the man you are. As for me, you can send me back to Denver. I hope you will. But you don't have the authority to fire me. Only Billy can do that. So if you want me gone, just say so. I'll be glad to leave. Otherwise shut the fuck up and let me do my job. A job, I might add, that you don't even understand, much less would be able to do. Now what is it? Do you want me to go back to Denver or not?"

"Well, I . . . I . . . never," Bartlett huffed.

"I expect that's the truth." Longarm turned on his heel and marched back out of the office.

Chapter 26

"I hear you got another taste of our marshal this morning," Loomis said over a cup of coffee several hours later.

"How'd you hear that?" Longarm asked.

"Bartlett was still ranting about it when I came back in," the chief deputy said with a grin.

Longarm raised an eyebrow.

"I had stepped out to go over to the post office, so I know that's when it had to have been." The grin faded and Loomis sighed. "I try to be loyal to the man. Really I do. After all, I owe the man my job and the loyalty that goes with it. But sometimes it isn't easy."

"I don't know how you do it," Longarm said. He almost added that he himself would not stand for such. In his opinion, no job was worth that sort of abuse. But then he did not know Mark Loomis's reasons for hanging on to his badge. And putting up with Jason Bartlett.

Loomis motioned to the counter man, and the fellow brought the coffeepot to refill their cups. When he had gone, Longarm reached into his pocket and produced the slip of paper with the list of names Carl Roberts had written down. He pushed the paper across the counter to Loomis. "Have you seen these? Know who any of them are?"

The local man leaned closer and looked them over carefully before shaking his head. "No. Who are they?"

Longarm explained how he had come by the names.

"Obviously they meant something to Carl but not to me." Loomis leaned back, picked up his cup, and drank, then carefully replaced it on the counter. "I should have thought to look through the house for clues to whatever Carl was working on. But I'll bet you can understand why he worked from home as much as possible. He didn't come in all that often. Most of the boys don't. Once they see the way things are around here, they stay away as much as they can."

Loomis's grin returned. "Then they quit."

"I can understand that," Longarm said.

Loomis eyed a glass dome with a pile of doughnuts under it. He hesitated for a minute or so, then gave in. "Give me one of those, Dave. And one for my partner here."

Longarm did not especially want a doughnut, but he did not want to be rude. And the puffy, sugar-frosted confection did taste good.

Chapter 27

Longarm found a dusty little store that advertised it sold 5- and 10-cent notions. Amid the clutter and junk inside he found a small note pad sized to fit inside a shirt pocket. He paid three cents for the pad and dropped it into a pocket.

He went back to his hotel to clean up—he did not have a change of clothes at Jenny's house and was feeling a bit clammy from wearing the same things too long—and get fresh clothing.

He sent his dirty clothes out to be laundered, then walked down the block to a barber shop. A shave and a trim left him feeling chipper.

From there he returned to the café that Mark Loomis patronized and took a table in the back corner.

"Coffee again, Marshal?" the counter man asked.

"Sure, why not. Dave, is it?"

"That's right. David Dwyer. This is my place," Dwyer said proudly.

"It's nice, Dave. Very nice. Say, I forgot t' buy a pencil. D'you have one I could borrow for a little while?"

"Sure thing, Marshal." Dwyer brought a pencil stub along with the coffee and placed both on the table.

The café owner returned to his counter while Longarm pulled out his note pad and list of names.

He carefully wrote each name on a separate sheet of paper, ending up with a thin sheaf of papers with only a single name written on each. He put them into a coat pocket. Then he put the master list containing all the names in his wallet along with some currency and his badge.

"Lunch, Marshal?" Dwyer asked.

Longarm blinked. "Is it that time already?" He had thought to take Jenny to lunch but she had to be at work in time for the lunch trade. Tomorrow, he told himself. He would take her out to eat tomorrow. In the meantime . . .

"What's the special today, Dave?"

Chapter 28

"Afternoon, Marshal. You want me to saddle your horse? You just set right over there. I'll have him ready for you in a jiffy."

"Thanks, Shorty," Longarm said with a smile. "Say, while I think about it, I'll bet you know most of the men who come through here. I'd expect they would stop here when they come to town no matter where they go on to do their drinking or their eating or their shopping."

Longarm pulled out his wallet and took out the master list of names he had found in Carl Roberts's desk. "Do you know any of these men, Shorty?"

The hostler politely took the piece of paper but he held it down by his side without so much as a glance at the names written on it.

"There's something I ought to tell you, Marshal. I, uh, I don't know my letters. Can't read a lick. I'm sorry."

"How's about if I read the names to you then?" Longarm suggested.

Shorty's expression brightened into a broad smile. "Sure, I can do that for you."

Longarm read out the names slowly, one by one. Shorty knew nearly all of them.

"Except for . . . what did you call the man . . . James Addison Ward? I don't know nobody like that. I know a fella name of Slim Ward. Could be the same man, but I don't know him by James Addison. Just Slim."

"Could you tell me about these fellows, please, Shorty?"

"All of 'em?"

"Yes, if you don't mind. Who they are and where they're from. Where I can find them," Longarm said. "Like that."

"Oh, I got the time if you're up to it, Marshal. But what about the bay?" Shorty already had the bay's bridle in hand.

"The bay can wait awhile. This list is more important," Longarm said. "Let's step outside so we can smoke. Don't want t' do it in your barn. Would you like a cigar, Shorty?"

"Well, now, normally I chew, but since you're offering." Shorty grinned and led the way behind the barn, where they could lean on the corral rails while Shorty spoke and Longarm wrote down whatever he knew about the names on Carl Roberts's list.

Chapter 29

By the time Longarm had all the information Shorty could give him, it was growing late in the afternoon, what with interruptions by people wanting to retrieve their own horses, rent a horse or a buggy or a heavy wagon.

Longarm did not regret the time spent. Not at all.

It also, he was pleased to note, kept him in town overnight. He walked over to the saloon where Jenny worked, took a table at the side of the room, and ordered a beer. Which Jenny brought.

"Are you free for a late dinner?" he asked. "An' maybe somethin' more afterward?"

Her smile would have been answer enough, but she compounded it by leaning down and giving him a kiss. "Pick me up when I get off work?" she said.

"Count on it," Longarm said, squeezing her hand. And remembering to pay for the beer. He did not want to stick Jenny with his bills, not even for something as small as a beer.

He sat long enough to drink the beer then wandered outside. With time on his hands, he did a little shopping for a shirt that struck his fancy and a more practical pair of balbriggans. He bought a string tie and a sack of tinned foods to carry along when he went on the road again. He had a grocer grind a quarter pound of coffee and ate a pickle. All in all a lazy afternoon.

Longarm smiled, wondering what that asshole Jace Bartlett would think of the way he was conducting this investigation. Not that he cared a whit.

Come evening he took his purchases back to the hotel and deposited them in his room. While he was there, he called for a tub and water to be brought up so he could bathe. He wanted, after all, to be nice and fresh in all the places where Jenny's tongue was likely to be later that evening.

And at the appointed time he showed up at the saloon ready to escort the lady.

"So tell me, ma'am, what is the nicest restaurant in town?" he asked.

"That would be the Azuras House. But I'm not dressed for anything like that," she said.

"You look good enough to me," he told her.

"They might not be serving at this hour."

"Now you're makin' excuses," Longarm said.

Jenny hesitated, then said, "I am, aren't I? I guess . . . I'm a little nervous. I've never been to the Azuras or anything like it."

"Well, I want you t' be comfortable," Longarm said. "The whole idea is t' please you, after all."

"Do you know what would really please me?"

"Tell me." He stopped walking. They stood on a street corner. A heavy dray and a pair of buggies drove by and a handful of pedestrians passed.

"I would like to go over to the bakery and buy some bread and cheese and go back to my house for a light supper. And maybe a bottle of wine. Like in the *Rubaiyat of Omar Khayyam*." She giggled. "A loaf of bread, a jug of wine, and you . . . It's a book of poetry from a long time ago. I've wanted . . . if you don't mind."

Longarm smiled. "Whatever pleases you."

Jenny's nose wrinkled in unspoken laughter. "Then afterward we can try again to get me pregnant. If, that is, if you don't mind."

"Reckon I can handle that part o' the evening anyway." Longarm laughed and took her arm. "Let's go do that shoppin'. But you'll have t' tell me where to get the makin's for this indoor picnic you have planned."

"Oh, Custis. An indoor picnic. That's an even better idea. We can do it on the living room floor. I'll spread a blanket and arrange some pillows."

"An' I can go out in your yard an' see can I rustle up some ants to make it just perfect."

She giggled and clutched his arm tight. "This way. We'll go to the bakery first. Then . . ."

Chapter 30

The picnic was a success. So was the evening afterward. Longarm and Jenny ended up on her living room floor, naked and sweaty and enjoying each other thoroughly.

"You are a good woman, Jennifer Roberts," Longarm declared at one point. And smiling, added, "An' you're a good fuck, too."

"Now that is the sort of compliment a girl can cherish," Jenny said, laughing.

"Always glad t' be of service," he said.

"And you have serviced me very nicely," she said. "Will you stay the night? We could do it again in the morning, you know. I don't have to be at work until late tomorrow."

"Oh, but I do. Got t' get moving. I need t' run down those names Carl left." Longarm got up off the floor and began looking around for his clothes, which were on the sofa mingled with hers.

"More wine before you go? Or anything?"

"Don't you start that or I won't get no sleep at all." He dressed then leaned down and kissed the girl. "Get some sleep an' build your strength for the next time," he said.

Jenny saw him to the door. He stood on her porch for a minute or so, enjoying the feel of the night air. He felt good. After a bit he lit a cheroot and made his way back to the hotel.

In the morning he was up early despite his late night with Jenny. He dressed quickly and went down the street to the café for a heavy breakfast, thinking the meal might have to last him through the day.

Shorty was busy, so Longarm saddled the bay himself and waved to the friendly hostler on his way out of the barn.

This time out, though, he was wary about his backtrail. Mildly uncomfortable about being hemmed in by trees and thick foliage after his years in the vast, open spaces of the West but careful, too, to look for any would-be ambusher like there had been the last time he rode out of town.

He saw nothing but could not escape the feeling that he was being watched.

Still, he had a job to do. That was what he was here for and never mind the pleasure he found in his dalliance with Jennifer Roberts.

Shorty had been able to point him in the general direction of some of his customers, but that only involved the direction they took when they drove away from the livery. He had not been able to give Longarm any firm information about where the people on the list lived or how to find them.

The first name on the list was D. Patterson. Shorty thought the man's first name was Dwight, but he was not sure about that. He lived southeast of Springfield, as in fact most of the men seemed to. Apparently that was an area that lent itself to the production of illegal whiskey.

Longarm already knew from his previous foray out into the countryside that the area was heavily forested and well watered. The land was choppy, with hidden dells and gulleys.

He followed the road Shorty said Patterson took when he left town until he came to a tiny crossroads store with a pump and trough out front. He stopped there and let the bay drink, then went inside.

"Help you, friend?" the elderly man behind the counter said.

"I'm lookin' for a fella," Longarm told him. "You might know him."

"I might."

"His name is Patterson."

"There's a heap of Pattersons hereabouts," the shopkeeper said. "Which of them would you be looking for? And why?"

"This Patterson uses the initial D. An' why I want t' talk with him is my affair an' his. Nobody else's," Longarm said.

The storekeeper nodded. "Not that it matters. I don't know 'im anyhow."

The man was lying. Longarm felt sure of that, but short of beating the information out of him, there seemed no way to change his mind. Except possibly one.

"It's worth a twenty-dollar double eagle to me t' get in touch with the man," Longarm said.

The storekeeper brightened and said, "Well, why di'nt you say so to begin with."

Chapter 31

It was a wagon track but one that was little used and almost overgrown. Longarm had to bend low over his saddle horn to keep the branches from sweeping his hat off as the bay walked softly down the path.

The path wound back and forth to keep from becoming too steep for a loaded wagon to drive through. At several points Longarm thought the intruding foliage might well have been deliberately encouraged to creep over the road.

He dropped down into a gulley and picked his way beside a thin stream. Ahead there was a pall of smoke lying close to the ground.

Longarm smiled. He could smell wood smoke and . . . something else as well.

He had found at least one of Carl's suspects, and they were indeed making whiskey.

The still was located on a bend of the creek. Hammered tin fashioned into a large cone with a curlicue spiral of tubing coming out of the top. Smears of flour paste sealing the cooker. Bags of mixed grains scattered about and barrels of grain being sprouted. Stacks of wood to feed the fire beneath the cooker. And jugs—a great many jugs—to hold the distilled product.

Even so, this was a small operation, probably a family-run thing. Certainly it was no threat to the commerce of the United States of America.

Longarm rode up to the still and reined the bay to a halt. He sat quiet, hands folded on the saddle horn, waiting.

He did not have long to wait.

"Hey! Who the hell are you?"

Longarm nodded and, with his left hand, touched the brim of his Stetson. His right remained where it was on the saddle horn, only a few inches from the butt of his .45. "I'm the fella who's gonna blow your ass t' Kingdom Come if you don't point that rifle in some other direction."

"Bullshit," the whiskey maker retorted. "I already got you covered." He was a young man, probably not out of his twenties, with a full beard and reddish brown hair. He wore bib overalls with flannel long johns underneath. The rifle in his hands was a Winchester or Marlin lever action; Longarm could not see which from where he sat on top of the bay horse.

"Ayuh," Longarm said calmly. "You got that shooter pointed my way. But I'd have you layin' on the ground bleeding your life out before you could get it in action. Trust me 'bout this. It's been tried before yet here I set."

"You're a cool one, I'll give you credit for that," the moonshiner said.

"Got reason t' be," Longarm responded. "I know what I can do an' what I can't. How 'bout you? How many gunfights you been in?"

The young man dropped the butt of his rifle—it was a Marlin, Longarm saw—to the ground. "Step down and state your business," he said.

"I'm here thinkin' to keep you from going t' prison," Longarm said.

"What the fuck?"

"Let me explain," Longarm said as he left the saddle.

Chapter 32

"Can I have a taste o' that product first? It's been a dry ride this morning," Longarm asked.

The moonshiner found a tin cup and wiped it out with his fingers then held the cup under the tubing to collect an inch or so of colorless whiskey.

Longarm tipped the cup up and sampled the man's wares. "Smooth," he said, coughing.

"It needs to age fifteen or twenty minutes," the fellow said.

"Yeah, I can tell." Longarm extended his hand and introduced himself.

"Dave Patterson," the moonshiner said.

"You're just the fella I been looking for," Longarm said.

"You said something about prison?" Patterson prompted.

Longarm finished off the whiskey Patterson just made. The inside of his mouth felt like it was collapsing in on itself. The man was right. It did need a bit of aging. "I did," Longarm said. He smiled and brought out his badge.

"Oh, shit," Patterson mumbled.

"Now it ain't all that bad," Longarm said. "I can see you

aren't into heavy production here an' you're tryin' to make a good product. I don't want t' bother you nor carry you off in chains. What I want is t' set and, um, visit a little. You know some things that I'd like you t' share with me." He smiled and hooked his thumbs into his gun belt. That was just in case Patterson reacted by bringing that Marlin up to bear.

"You aren't gonna arrest me?" Patterson asked.

"Furthest thing from my mind," Longarm told him.

"But you want to talk."

Longarm nodded.

"About what, exactly?"

"About some folks around here who are making large quantities of very poorly made whiskey. The stuff could kill people, an' we can't have that, can we." Longarm carefully avoided mentioning the federal tax on whiskey since Patterson quite obviously was not paying it either. "I suspect you'd know who I'm talking about."

Patterson peered off into the distance in thought. But he left the rifle butt on the ground. After a minute or so he helped himself to a sample of his own product and offered Longarm another taste, which Longarm accepted.

"Don't know of any son of a bitch revenuer who drinks corn with his prisoners," Patterson observed.

"You ain't a prisoner," Longarm said. "Just a fella that knows things I'd like him t' share with me." He drank the offered whiskey. It went down smoother this time than the first taste had done.

"Come set down then." Patterson looked up the hillside and waved, then he turned to Longarm with a grin. "You been under my pap's gun sights since the minute you rode in."

"He's good," Longarm said. "I never saw him."

Patterson chuckled. "Yeah, he's a sneaky old son of a bitch, all right."

Patterson Sr. came down the hill thrashing and crashing through the brush. He held a battered old Springfield musket that looked like it had been through several wars, not just one.

The father was a gray and older version of the son. "I'm Dwight," he introduced himself.

"Custis Long," Longarm said.

"Mr. Long is a U.S. marshal," the son said to his father. "But he came to ask us some questions instead of to arrest us."

Patterson Sr. nodded, obviously accepting his son's evaluation of their guest. "Come along then," he said. "We'll talk."

Chapter 33

Longarm accepted another cup of moonshine, this one poured from a wooden keg. It was smooth and delightful on the tongue and in the belly.

"You're not drinking?" he asked when neither of his hosts joined him.

The elder Patterson grinned, exposing several gaps where teeth should have been. "Never touch the stuff," he said.

"Wise man," Longarm returned. "But I'll enjoy my debauchery a little while longer if you don't mind. This batch, by the way, is excellent."

"Double run," Patterson Sr. said. "And no sugar ever. It's the only way."

"It's a craftsman's way," Longarm said.

"Son, go fetch Mr. Long a jug of the good stuff, seeing as how he's a man that enjoys his whiskey."

Patterson Jr. got up and left the stacks of grain sacks where they were sitting. He returned moments later with a crockery jug that he handed to Longarm. "Our best," he said. "Not that it isn't all good. Pop knows what he's doing. But some comes out better than others. This is the best."

"Like I told you," Longarm said, "I'm looking for the fellows who are producing large amounts of bad whiskey. It's them that I want, not you small producers. And if you don't mind me mentioning the obvious, if I take them down, it decreases your competition. I suspect they're flooding the market as it is. Help me get rid of them and it gets rid of some of your competitors."

"It wouldn't be right for me to give you any names," Senior said.

"I'm not asking for that," Longarm said. "Not exactly. What I have already is a list of names. That's how I found you. I'd like you to look at that list and cross off any names that you think don't belong there. Like yours, for instance."

"Excuse us for a minute?" Patterson Sr. said.

"Of course," Longarm told him.

Without asking, Patterson Jr. took Longarm's cup and refilled it with the good stuff—which was very good indeed—then followed his father out of sight.

Longarm guessed the two were gone for five minutes or more, obviously talking over the lawman's request. When they returned, they handed Longarm his slip of paper.

Most of the names on it, including their own, had been crossed off.

"Would it be proper for me t' ask where I can go about finding these fellas?" Longarm asked.

"It would not. And do keep in mind, please, that we have told you nothing," the elder Patterson said.

"Gentlemen," Longarm said, rising and handing his empty cup back to Junior, "I bid you a very good day. An' when I write up any reports, I will keep in mind that neither of you actually told me anything."

He touched the brim of his Stetson—with his right hand this time—and went back to the bay horse.

Chapter 34

"Sorry, mister. I mean, well, I could use another of those double eagles, but I don't know where any of these fellows live. This one"—the storekeeper pointed to a name on the list Longarm carried—"this one I think has been in here. But I couldn't say that I know him and don't know where he lives. Not around here, though. I'm sure of that."

Longarm thanked the man and bought a drink of white whiskey in order to stay on the fellow's good side just in case he could he helpful in the future. He did not have to know that Longarm was a lawman. It would be much to the better if he did not.

Nightfall found Longarm far from any settlement that he knew about. A village might have been just around the next bend, but he was not going to keep pushing in search of a proper bed to lie in. He had been sleeping on the ground for a good portion of his lifetime and was not going to worry about it now.

He found a pleasant spot beside one of the many streams that flowed through this country and unsaddled the bay horse. He had not brought any hobbles and knew better than to turn a rented horse loose to graze. The darn thing would head for home and he would be left afoot if he were that foolish.

Instead he let the animal graze for half an hour or so while he held it on a lead rope, then he tied the bay to a sturdy gum tree. That would do for the night, he figured, and he could let it graze a little more in the morning.

When he came to a village in the morning, he could buy some grain for the bay. And something for himself as well.

He had not brought provisions for his own comforts overnight either. But then he was not out here with comfort in mind.

Longarm chose a patch of lush grass and placed his saddle at one side of it. The saddle would do for a pillow and the saddle blanket to cover him from the night air.

Supper consisted of a handful of jerky—he did not know what meat it was made from and probably was happier not knowing—and a drink from the creek.

A small fire kept his thoughts company until sleep tugged at his eyelids. He stretched out with the scent of crushed grass pleasant in his nostrils and pulled the saddle blanket over him to ward off any dew that might collect during the night.

He was asleep within seconds.

Chapter 35

Longarm was already reaching for his .45 when he awakened. Something in the night was not right. The night sounds . . . crickets, tree frogs, squirrels, whatever . . . were not as they should be.

And other sounds intruded.

Footfalls? He thought so. The faint sounds seemed like someone walking, like cloth pant legs brushing each other? Could be.

Longarm had not lived this long by ignoring faint warnings. A sense of warning in his gut was enough to worry him, that or even a premonition. Whatever the cause, if any, he took a firm grip on his revolver and slid out from under the saddle blanket he had been using as a cover against the night air.

As silently as he could, he crawled belly down through the lush grass that grew beside the creek. He reached a stand of sumac and slithered inside its protection.

Only then did he rise into a sitting position, peering into the clearing with the .45 in hand. His saddle, hat, blanket, and boots remained where he had lain down to sleep. They were much too flat to have the appearance of a sleeping man, but they would just have to do.

Longarm waited, a patient hunter ready for prey.

He listened to the bay horse cropping grass, tearing the blades from the ground and noisily chewing.

Then the horse stopped grazing and lifted its head, ears pointed toward the creek.

Someone was there. Longarm was sure of it.

He shifted his eyes slightly away from what he wanted to see, an old trick that sometimes helped. And sometimes did not.

This time it enabled him to make out two shadowy figures moving in the night.

The two separated, one moving in ghostly silence toward the bay, the other creeping stealthily toward Longarm's saddle and blanket.

Longarm could not see if the two were armed. He assumed they were. He had every right to let fly with the .45 and put the two down and dead.

Instead he waited, giving them time to hang themselves if that was what they wanted.

The one by the horse took the bay by the reins. The one by the fake sleeper raised his hands.

And struck.

He smashed Longarm's hat with something hard and heavy then stood upright, proud of himself.

"I got 'im, Hennie."

"Good fer you, Ralph."

Longarm's expression was grim when he stood and moved out from the sumac.

"You got shit," he declared, cocking the .45, that faint sound loud in the silence of the night.

Chapter 36

"Oh, Jesus," one of the men mumbled.

"You shoulda thought o' Him before you went an' fucked up, not after," Longarm said.

"P-Please don't shoot," the other one said, the tremor in his voice suggesting that he had begun to cry.

The two presented Longarm with a problem. He was too far from Springfield to easily take the pair back for trial there. And he did not really trust the local law to keep quiet about him being a deputy United States marshal. That was something he was trying not to reveal until or unless he wanted it known.

He compromised.

"Strip," he said.

"What?"

"Strip, I said. All your clothes. On the ground. Now!"

"Mister, we're a long ways from home. Tha's why we was gonna take your horse. Just for a ride home, y' see. Only a ride," one of them whined.

"An' what part of that ride meant you had t' kill me first?" Longarm demanded.

"Oh, we wasn't—"

"Listen t' me, shit-for-brains, I stood right here an' watched you try an' bash my brains out with that . . . what is that thing anyway?" Longarm said.

"Oh, it's just a stick I picked up. That's all."

"Drop it."

The nearer one dropped his cudgel. And followed it to the ground, dropping to his knees to plead his case.

"Mister, please, we—"

"You got caught is what it is," Longarm said. He took a long step closer to the one who minutes earlier had tried to beat his brains out. The Colt in his hand flashed and the would-be robber cried out. The front sight on Longarm's .45 had slashed across his face, opening up a long gash that began to bleed copiously.

"You," Longarm said to the other one. "On your fucking knees, you son of a bitch."

"Mister, please. I never tried to hurt you none. Please don't," that one whined.

Longarm shoved his .45 back into his holster, took three steps toward the second robber, and kicked the man square in the balls. The fellow grunted in pain and dropped to the ground writhing.

Longarm gave the two of them time to recover a little, the first one to stanch the bleeding on his cheek and upper lip, the second one to straighten up and get his breath back.

"Now get your asses gone," he snarled. "If I see either one o' you stupid bastards again, I'll shoot you down like dogs." Not that he likely would recognize them again in daylight. But they did not have to know that.

He did not have to say it twice. Both robbers hobbled away as quickly as they were able.

Longarm waited until they were beyond his hearing, then hunkered down and began collecting his few things. He did not really think the pair would come back and try again . . . but he was not going to bet his life on it.

Thanks to them, he was done sleeping for the night, so he quickly reshaped his crushed hat, pulled on his boots, and gathered up his saddle and blanket.

He spoke softly to the bay so it would not be startled by his approach in the night and got ready to ride.

"Bastards," he grumbled aloud as he swung into the saddle. "Disturbin' a man's sleep. Huh!"

He heeled the bay into motion.

Chapter 37

He found a tiny crossroads store, where he bought a meal and enough supplies for another two days, but the old fellow who ran the place denied knowing the men Longarm wanted to find. He could even have been telling the truth.

The store did not sell cheroots but they did have some slightly stale panatelas and some crooks that were practically dripping in cherry brandy. Longarm took the panatelas. The mere thought of smoking a cherry brandy–soaked cigar was enough to turn his stomach.

Longarm took his newly acquired supplies, thanked the proprietor, and left. There was something about the place that he did not trust. It was nothing he could put his finger on, just a feeling of unease.

He nooned in a shaded grove then rode on, stopping whenever he could find a farm to ask about one of the men on his list. It was likely that the people he talked to knew at least one of the men, but to a man they denied any knowledge of the moonshiners.

Whether that was because of loyalty or fear or simply stubborn bloody-mindedness, Longarm had no way to tell.

But then strangers asking questions were not likely to accomplish much, not here nor much of anywhere.

It was nearing evening when he got to thinking about that and realized the error in his thinking.

Of course. He was a stranger here. There was no reason the locals should want to help.

With a shake of his head at his own folly, Longarm put the spurs to the bay horse and headed out at a swift lope heading for the Richardsons' ramshackle farm.

The Richardson brothers knew him. Or thought they did, believing him to be an outlaw of some kind and a hard-ass son of a bitch at that.

The boys were very likely to give him the lead he needed.

Chapter 38

Night caught him well short of the Richardson place so he stopped at an inn that called itself Valhalla.

"I'm needin' a room," Longarm told the fellow who came in answer to the bell over the door. "An' what accommodation do you have for my horse?"

"There's a shed out back and grass hay. You can put the horse up there. I got no grain for it, though."

"He can make do with the hay," Longarm said. "I'll go see to him now, be back in directly. Can you feed me supper or do I need t' handle that on my own?"

"I'll have something ready for you when you get done with the horse."

Longarm nodded and went back outside. He led the bay around behind the single-story inn and into a stall in the promised shed. He stripped the tack off the animal and gave it an armful of clean hay then gave the bay a rubdown, checked its feet, and made sure it was reasonably secure in the stall.

He left saddle and bridle there but carried his saddlebags into the inn with him.

The promised meal was a stew, long on potatoes but short on meat. It was, however, warm and filling. And it was better than trail rations. Longarm had no complaint.

"Your room is the last one back," the clerk/waiter/proprietor told him. "The hallway is over there. Just follow it back all the way. You're on the left."

Longarm thanked the man, picked up his saddlebags, and followed the directions to a room that was small and poorly furnished but seemed clean enough.

There was no lamp but a stub of candle provided enough light for him to crawl gratefully onto the bed.

He considered stripping down and washing with a splash from the pitcher but was just too tired to bother. Perhaps in the morning, he told himself.

He removed his gun belt and placed the .45 under the thin pad that served as a pillow, placed his Stetson on the floor since there was no bedside table, kicked his boots off, and let them lie where they fell. He blew out the candle and closed his eyes.

He usually was able to sleep almost instantly. Not this night. He tossed and turned, trying to find a cool spot on the thin pillow.

That may have saved his life.

Chapter 39

Longarm lay awake, wishing he had thought to bring a bottle along on the trip this time. Tomorrow he would buy one. But that would be tomorrow. Small comfort tonight.

He lay on his back, eyes wide open. He noticed a change in the faint light beyond the window. There was a quarter moon. Between that and the stars there was enough light to flood the window with a thin, gray light.

There was no glass in the window. Rough but not unheard of in the countryside far from city lights. Nor were there any curtains although a sheet of muslin would have provided some privacy.

Now Longarm could see that faint disturbance of light.

He rolled onto his side in time to see a stealthy figure standing in the window frame.

The man seemed to be pointing something . . .

Longarm slid off the side of the bed and crouched on the floor, reaching for his .45. Just in case something . . .

The bright light of fire blossomed at the window, and the room was filled with the roar of a powerful gunshot, then an acrid stink of exploded gunpowder in close quarters.

A load of shot struck the bed where Longarm had been lying.

The lighter report of his .45 followed close behind the shotgun blast. Longarm fired twice and dropped flat.

He was blinded by the muzzle flashes and deafened by the concussion of the gunshots. He worked his jaw frantically, trying to restore his hearing. He never had any idea if that worked, but he always tried it regardless.

The window frame remained empty after the brief, violent flurry of smoke and noise.

Longarm waited until his hearing returned, then crept across the bare floorboards to crouch beneath the window. He was not sure but he thought he heard . . . something. Gurgling, sort of.

Only when that faint sound ended did he rise a little and peer outside.

On the ground beside the window he could see a body.

It was odd, he thought, that the proprietor had not come to see what the shooting had been about.

Odd. Or sensible.

A man who runs to a gunshot is either a law officer or a damn fool. Apparently the hotel man was neither of those.

Longarm gave the son of a bitch outside time enough to do his dying, then went back to his bedside and lit the candle. He carried it to the window and leaned down.

That explained why the clerk had not come running. The dead man on the ground outside was the desk clerk who had checked him in a little earlier.

Longarm considered gathering his things and leaving, but he was just too damned tired. He went back to bed, and this time he was able to drop off to sleep without a problem.

Chapter 40

He slept until past daybreak then rose and splashed some cold water on his whiskers. He had no idea where he might find a barber, and anyway the growth of beard might help to give him the wild and uncurried look of an outlaw on the run.

He walked over to the window and peered out. The dead clerk was still lying there. No one had come running to see what the shooting was about and no one had bothered to cart the dead man away. Longarm did not even know who to report the death to.

With a grunt, he pulled out a cigar and bit the twist off. He spat the twist out the window, not intentionally on the dead man who had tried to kill him but in that direction. He lit the cigar and tossed the spent match out the window, too.

He was already dressed so he gathered up the few things he had brought in with him and went back out to the shed, saddled the bay horse, and went on down the road in search of breakfast.

Half a day and several false starts later he found the Richardson farm.

"You boys aren't so easy to find," Longarm told the brother who stepped out to greet him. He assumed the others were somewhere nearby where they could hold their guns on him. "Billy, isn't it?"

"That I am, Mr. Long." Billy grinned, showing a gap or two where teeth should have been. "You remembered."

"Ayuh. I came t' set with you boys, maybe have a meal an' a drink, maybe get your advice about somethin'."

"Well, climb down off that horse then an' welcome, Mr. Long." Billy must have given some signal although Longarm could not see what it might have been. Whatever it was, the other two stepped out of hiding, guns in hand, and came to greet their guest.

"Welcome, Mr. Long."

"Good to see you again, Mr. Long."

"Would you like a cup of the good stuff, Mr. Long?"

"Pleased to meet you, Mr. Long," the fourth brother, Thomas, said.

Longarm chuckled and said, "Traveling can be dry work, an' a taste o' your finest would go a long way toward clearing the dust outa my throat."

The whiskey was as good as he remembered, and the food the brothers offered was plain but filling. Both were indeed welcome after the ride.

"How is the law around here?" he asked over the rim of his cup. "I had something of a problem at the place where I stayed last night, an' I'm wondering if someone will be comin' after me for it."

"You got nothing to worry about as long as you're with one of us," Jesse said. "We got the law in our pocket."

Leroy nodded agreement. "Nothing to worry about," he said.

"That's a relief," Longarm said with a smile. "I got troubles enough without that, too. Say, you wouldn't have any more o' that good whiskey, would you? It goes down so smooth it just asks for more."

He had another cup. Or two. Then said, "There's something I got in mind that maybe you boys could help me with."

"Sure, Mr. Long, we'll be glad to help out if we can," Thomas told him.

Longarm pulled out his list.

Chapter 41

"Uh, sorry," Leroy said, handing the list back.

"You don't know any of them? Damn!" Longarm said.

"It isn't that. Mayhap we do know them. It's that we can't read," Billy told him.

"None o' you?"

"No. Is that a problem?"

"Not for me it ain't. How's about if I read the list out loud," Longarm said.

"Oh, we got good memory. That oughta do."

Among them the brothers knew all the men on the list but one. "Good old boys," they said. "The most of 'em make cheap whiskey for Mr. Howard."

"What d'you mean by 'cheap whiskey'? An' who is Mr. Howard?" Longarm asked.

Leroy leaned forward and lowered his voice as if to keep anyone from overhearing what he was about to say. "Mr. Howard is the fella that came through here a year, year and a half ago and started buying cheap-made white whiskey. It don't have to be good. There just has to be a lot of it. You make the good stuff by using natural grains and running the product through the still twicet. That's why it's called double run. That's what we been giving you. Smooth and nice, yes? Well, the cheap whiskey that Mr. Howard wants to buy you make by fermenting your grain with sugar and running it through just the once. It comes out powerful but harsh. That cheap stuff is what Mr. Howard wants, and he'll buy all of it he can get his hands on. Doesn't matter if it's bad whiskey, just so there's a lot of it."

"That's interesting," Longarm said. "Who is Mr. Howard?"

"He's a gentleman from up the Missoura somewheres. Has his own steamboat. Comes through twicet a year to buy all he can get."

"Any idea what he does with it?" Longarm asked.

All three of the brothers shook their heads. "He comes through in wagons. Buys the whiskey and goes . . . someplace else. Over to the river, I'd guess."

"The river?"

"You know. The Miss'ippi," Jesse said.

"Oh, that river."

"We done said Mr. Howard has him a steamboat. We loads it up spring and fall and takes all that whiskey north."

"You're sure about that? North?"

"Oh, yeah. We heard him talk now an' then. He takes boatloads twicet each year. Must carry a thousand gallons or more. Doesn't matter if it's any good, just so there's lots of it."

"Now that's mighty interestin'," Longarm mused over a cup of the good stuff. "North."

Illegal, non-tax-paid whiskey by the boatload. Literally. Carried north to . . . where?

There were thousands of possible destinations, but the one that made Longarm's blood run cold was also the place where a trader in illicit whiskey could make the most profit. This Mr. Howard could well be supplying the wild tribes with whiskey.

And large quantities of raw whiskey, sold illegally like that, could incite the tribes to violence.

It was Longarm's experience that the kindest and most pleasant Indian could become a raging maniac if you poured enough liquor into him. It was a reluctant conclusion but one painfully learned.

Of course, this Howard person could simply be supplying roadhouses and legitimate mercantiles.

But if that were the case, then surely quality would play a part in Howard's equation.

"I want t' meet this Mr. Howard," Longarm said. "Maybe him an' me can do some business. Will you introduce us?"

"Glad to, Mr. Long," Thomas, who seemed to be the oldest of the brothers, told him, "but Mr. Howard won't be here for another week or so. We heard he's down-country now, working his way up here. But he won't be here for a spell. At least a week. We never know what his schedule might be, just that he'll get to us when he gets here, him and his wagons."

"He travels with wagons?"

Billy nodded. "To haul all the liquor he buys."

"Then I'll come back next week," Longarm said. "You boys can make the introductions. It may be worth something to you."

"We can do that, Mr. Long," Leroy said. "We can sure do that."

Longarm nodded, thanked the boys for the liquor, and returned to the bay horse.

Next week, he was thinking.

But—change of plan—there would be no introductions. He had something else in mind now.

Chapter 42

Longarm returned the bay horse to Shorty and headed for Mrs. Canfield's rooming house. Once there, he grabbed a change of clothing and headed for the barber shop, where he thoroughly enjoyed a bath and a shave, changed into the clean clothes, and dropped the soiled ones off at a laundry.

Then, smelling human again and looking about as good as he ever did manage, he headed for the saloon where Jenny worked.

The girl's smile was broad when he walked in.

"It's good to see you back, Custis," she said, bringing him a beer and a shot without being asked.

"I have a favor t' ask of you," he told the girl.

"Of course. Anything." She laughed. "You can ask anything, that is. I'm not saying I will want to give whatever it is that you want."

"I need a place t' lay low for a few days," he said. He downed the shot and followed it with a swallow of the crisp, fresh beer. "Truth is, I want t' stay out of Jace

Bartlett's sight. I'll do my job, but I don't like that man an' don't want him ordering me around."

"You want to stay with me?" she said.

Longarm nodded and took another pull at the beer. "That I do."

Jenny's answer was a broad, happy grin.

Longarm threw his head back and laughed. "It's a lucky man that I am, Miss Jenny," he said. "Does, uh, does everyone think that I'm your boyfriend now?"

"Yes, they do. I made sure of it. Why?"

"Because," he said, putting an arm around her waist and drawing her near, "because I want t' kiss you, little lady."

She giggled. "And other things, I hope."

"We'll talk 'bout that later. For now"—he gave her a playful slap on the butt—"bring me another shot and a beer."

Jenny squealed and rose onto tiptoes in response to the slap. Then she hurried away to bring the shot and the beer.

Chapter 43

Longarm got his things from the rented room and moved them over to Jenny's house. She did not keep her front door locked so he let himself in, built a fire in the kitchen range, and had coffee waiting for her when she got home.

"Do you mind?" he asked.

"Not at all." She kissed him, a brief peck at first that turned into an attempt to push her tongue down his throat. And nearly succeeded.

"Whew!" Longarm muttered when the girl finally backed off. "We should do this more often."

"I agree," Jenny said. "But first, dear heart, is that coffee I smell?"

"Sit down an' get off your feet. I'll fetch you a cup. I got to admit, though. I'm no hand when it comes t' cooking. I don't have supper ready for you."

"The coffee is more than I ever expected," Jenny said, shedding clothes as she headed back to the bedroom.

When she emerged a few minutes later, she wore only the flimsy dressing gown that Longarm remembered. She had nothing underneath it.

"Nice," he said, handing her the cup of coffee he had ready for her.

"Will you be able to stay long?" she asked, peeping over the rim of the cup.

"Five days," he said.

Jenny's broad smile was answer enough.

Half an hour later Jenny stacked their supper dishes in the dry sink and turned to him. She let the dressing gown slide off her shoulders to the floor.

"Lovely," he said, and meant it.

"Pretty is as pretty does," Jenny said. "Come to bed now." She held out her hand and took his then led him into the bedroom.

She lay on the bed, thighs already parted. She fingered herself while Longarm quickly undressed.

He had an erection long before he got rid of the last of his clothing. Once he was naked, he joined her on the bed. Jenny's skin felt cool against his. He lay next to her, took her into his arms, and kissed her.

"I want to feel you inside me," she whispered.

"Always glad t' oblige," Longarm returned, laughing.

He moved on top of her and Jenny opened her legs and raised her hips to allow him entry into her wet, slippery pussy.

Longarm plunged deep inside Jenny's slim body. She held him close with her arms and with her legs and began pumping her hips eagerly. Within seconds she bit her lip and squealed as she reached her first climax.

He held back, enjoying the feeling of being inside her, until Jenny had come several more times. Then Longarm allowed himself his own release, his hot cum spewing into her.

Still she held on to him, holding him inside her, until her racing heartbeat returned to normal.

Then she kissed him. "Thank you," she whispered.

Chapter 44

The following Monday morning, Longarm saddled the bay horse and headed for the Richardsons' place, this time not having to search out the way.

Half an hour outside of town, though, he reined off the road and into a thick copse of pine trees mixed with sumac and wild cherry. He rode behind a screen of greenery . . . and waited.

Within minutes he had a visitor although not the one he expected. Longarm gigged the bay forward, breaking out of the trees to the roadway nearby.

"Good mornin' there, Shorty. Going hunting, are you?" He nodded toward the lever-action rifle, almost as long as Shorty was tall, that the little hostler was carrying over the pommel of his saddle.

Shorty blanched as pale as a sheet of foolscap. His rifle was pointed toward the far side of the road, and it would have taken a desperate and foolhardy gamble for him to try to swing it around and aim it toward Longarm.

"I . . . no, I'm not hunting anything," Shorty said. "I just happen to have the gun with me."

"An' I believe that, o' course," Longarm said, his voice and expression friendly. "Trouble is, I know what you been hunting. I'm surprised, though. I thought you was a friendly sort. Never knew you was lookin' for extra pay by shooting folks in the back. Tell me, though. Are you the one as killed Carl Roberts?"

"No, I . . . I never killed anybody," Shorty stammered.

"An' I suppose you ain't the one tried to backshoot me a little while back," Longarm said.

"No, I never."

"Then it's your tough luck that I'm gonna arrest your ass an' charge you with attempted murder of a law officer. Now hand over the rifle. Do it easy an' you'll live to serve out your prison time."

Longarm sidestepped the bay over beside Shorty's mount and reached out to take the rifle.

Shorty hesitated. It was easy enough to see the thought processes that passed through his mind in those seconds. Could he bring the long barrel of the rifle around to bear on a target on the wrong side of his horse?

The answer, which Shorty arrived at after only brief consideration, was that, no, he could not. Not, at least, quickly enough to keep Longarm from putting a bullet into him.

"Sure, Marshal. Here you go." He handed over the weapon, a very nice .38-55 with long-range sights, and held his wrists out for Longarm to apply handcuffs.

"I'll take you back t' town, Shorty, an' put you behind bars 'til I'm ready to testify a'gin you. It would go a long way toward helpin' you if you was to have a little chat with me on the way back. 'Bout things like who you're working for an' what they're up to . . . though I suspect I already know some of it. But you tell me anyway, just t' make sure I've got it right. Is that all right with you, Shorty?"

Shorty looked about as crestfallen and miserable as a human person could.

On the way back to town, he did have that little chat with Longarm. It confirmed some things. And surprised with others.

Chapter 45

Longarm made camp overseeing the road to the Richardson place but avoided riding in there. The brothers knew
him by his real name, and he did not want Mr. Howard to
hear that name. Considering the business he was in—and
where he plied that trade—the man might well have heard
about a United States marshal named Custis Long. Longarm did want to meet Howard but not under his own name.

So he holed up where he could keep an eye on the road.
And waited.

On the third day he saw Howard. Could hardly have
missed him.

The man traveled with a train of heavy freight wagons,
collecting liquor along the way. Longarm estimated each
wagon could hold perhaps a hundred gallons of illegal
whiskey underneath the protective covering of heavy tar-
paulins that should keep prying eyes from seeing what the
cargo was.

There were fourteen wagons in the train, each pulled by
two spans of oxen. It made for an impressive showing,
Longarm conceded.

Howard's personal wagon was essentially a sheepherder's wagon. It was easily identifiable by way of the stovepipe sticking through the canvas roof and the steps and low doorway at the rear. That wagon was pulled by a four-up of heavy horses. Clydsdales, Longarm thought. Big, powerful, extremely handsome animals, they were.

He watched them while they stopped on the road then one wagon detached itself from the train and took the poorly marked track down to the Richardson farm, Howard's lighter rig leading the way.

They were gone more than an hour then rejoined the train, which had been waiting, the oxen patient, the drivers less so.

The men gambled, spat, and drank while they were waiting.

Longarm just watched, his patience that of a hunter waiting for his prey to appear.

In fact, his prey already had appeared. Now he only had to work out how to go about taking it down.

Chapter 46

Longarm let the wagon train get several miles ahead before he mounted the bay horse and slowly followed at a slow, deliberate pace that should not close the gap.

Toward nightfall he increased the bay's gait and soon came in sight of the train, stopped now in a broad field close to a small river. This time he rode boldly into the camp.

Men were gathered around half a dozen campfires, talking and relaxing after the day's work. Longarm rode up to a fire close to Howard's wagon. The men at that fire, unlike the wagon drivers at the other fires, carried revolvers on their hips. He assumed these would be Howard's bodyguards. After all, the man seemed to be distributing money by the fistful. That meant his personal wagon probably contained a large quantity of cash, and that would indicate a need for bodyguards.

Longarm rode close to the fire where the bodyguards lounged. He dismounted and tied the bay to a wheel on one of the whiskey wagons. When he was close to the wagon, he could smell the harsh alcohol.

He chose a bodyguard more or less at random and walked up to the man.

"You're a cheat an' a liar," Longarm declared in a loud voice. He had no idea who the man was or what sort of person but figured he needed to showcase his talents.

The man Longarm addressed jumped to his feet. "Mister, I don't know you. You got the wrong man here," he declared. He was right about that, but Longarm was not about to admit to it.

"Wrong man, my ass," Longarm said. And punched him square in the jaw.

The fellow went down like a poleaxed steer. That was more than Longarm wanted. He did not want the fellow out cold. He wanted him up and swinging.

One of the man's companions, all of whom were on their feet now, stepped in to defend his friend.

Longarm punched him and knocked him flat as well, but this one bounced up almost immediately and started fighting.

Longarm slipped inside the fellow's roundhouse blows, bent over in a crouch, and started raining body blows into the fellow's midsection.

The first man crawled to his feet then and threw a punch. Longarm knocked it aside and drove a hard right low into the fellow's belly while the other one punched Longarm in the gut. Longarm turned his attention back to that one, knocked him down, then blocked another series of blows from the first man.

"That was my woman you was messin' with," Longarm snarled.

Both men dropped their fists and stepped back. "Woman? What woman? I ain't had no woman since we left Cape Girardeau."

Longarm paused. "You haven't? Are you sure 'bout that?"

"Of course I'm sure. Good Lord, man, you think I'd forget being without pussy for that long?"

"You aren't Dave Johnston?" Longarm rasped.

"No, I'm Bern Adams," the fellow said.

"Well, shit," Longarm exclaimed. "I've gone an' made a mistake here, I'm sorry t' tell you. I apologize." He held out his hand and the more than slightly confused fellow shook it.

"D'you happen to know Johnston?" he asked.

"Never heard of him," Adams said.

"Then d'you know where a man could get a bite t' eat and maybe find a job o' work to do?" Longarm asked.

Adams peered closely at Longarm for a moment, then said, "From the way you carry that pistol on your belly, you might know something about guns and how to use them. The boss might have a place for you if you ain't picky about what sort of work you do."

"I'll do most anything," Longarm said.

"What's your name, mister?"

"John Short," Longarm said.

"I'll go talk to the boss about you, Short," Adams said. "Meantime set down to our fire. Grab a couple of those biscuits and some chunks of meat. I'll be right back."

Longarm hunkered down beside the fire, his back deliberately toward the wagon where he expected Howard to be.

Chapter 47

"You are Short, I take it?" a voice behind him said.

Longarm stood, turned, faced a very large man with a walrus mustache and portly belly. "I am, sir."

The man extended his hand to shake. "Howard Butler," he said, so "Mr. Howard" had been somewhat misleading. "Adams tells me you might be a fighting man, Mr. Short."

Longarm nodded. "I been known to."

"My first question is: Are you loyal to the brand?" Butler said. "Will you stand by your employer if lead starts flying?"

"Been known t' do that, too," Longarm said with another nod.

"Do you have any scruples when it comes to Indians?" Butler asked.

Longarm turned his head and spat. "I got nothing t' say about them red sons o' bitches 'cept they all o' them ought t' die screaming on their way to Hell."

Butler looked at one of the men who had not

participated in the fight earlier. "Put Mr. Short to work, Johnson. Standard wage."

"Through to Cape Girardeau or beyond, Mr. Butler, sir?"

"I will determine that when I see how he performs," Butler said. The boss pivoted on his· heels—in a very military manner—and returned to his little house on wheels.

The man he had called Johnson stood and brushed himself off. He beckoned Longarm aside.

"The boss says you're in, and he is the boss. But don't cross me," Johnson warned. "Nor him. The pay is two dollars and a half a day. Bonuses if there is trouble and you handle yourself. You have a horse, I see. There's a picket rope over yonder." He pointed. "Put your animal with the others. All the feed he needs. Or you. All the ammunition, too," he added with a grin.

"There might be trouble?" Longarm asked.

"There most generally is. The boss is rich. Fools think they can take his money. They can't. Which is why us fellows are along. We guard the boss. More important, see, we guard the boss's wagon. Nobody goes in there but him. Nobody. Understand?"

Longarm nodded.

"Understand? You got to say it."

"I understand. Nobody in or out except him," Longarm said.

"What I want you to do is act as an outrider. Look for anybody that doesn't fit in, anybody that's nervous or heavy armed or you just think doesn't look right. If there's trouble, I want to see you in the thick of it. Understand?"

"I understand," Longarm repeated.

"Good. Throw your gear under that wagon over there and take your horse over to the picket rope. The cook wagon is two outfits back. Tell Jimbo I said to give you supper. All right?"

"All right," Longarm said.

"Go on now. And don't let your horse stir up dust when he goes by. The boss hates that."

Longarm nodded and returned to the bay, untied it from the wagon wheel, and led it off into the darkness in search of the picket line.

Chapter 48

Fourteen wagons, probably two dozen men . . . it seemed a bit much for one man to arrest. Besides, Longarm thought with a wry grin, he didn't have two dozen sets of handcuffs with him. He was not even sure he could round up that many if he collected every pair of 'cuffs available in the district.

More important, he wanted to make sure that Howard Butler was the big boss. There could well be someone above him in the hierarchy of this huge whiskey enterprise. That was something Longarm definitely wanted to determine before he announced himself and started making arrests.

And there was almost certainly someone else involved at the other end of the business. Longarm wanted him, or them, too.

He suspected—but did not yet know for certain—that the illegal whiskey was intended for sale to Indians somewhere up the Mississippi River. That, too, was illegal, and as a Federal officer, it was his duty to stop any such whiskey trade.

As a member of the train he saw everything but said nothing. Questions would not have been welcome, so he asked none.

He did, however, keep careful mental note of all the places they stopped to buy whiskey. When this was over, he intended to bring Mark Loomis back along with whatever other deputies they could muster to break up those stills and arrest the whiskey makers. Including the Richardson brothers, hospitable though they had been. He rather liked the boys, but it was a question of law and duty.

Of course, he could always forget the way to their particular operation.

In the meantime, he acted as one of Howard Butler's bodyguards.

And on his third day on the job he earned his two dollars and fifty cents.

Chapter 49

"Trouble," Longarm said, riding in from his post ahead of the train.

"You're sure?" the ramrod, Jim Johnson, asked.

"No, I ain't sure, but you said I should follow my gut 'bout these things. An' of a sudden I got a bad feeling."

Johnson and the other guards were riding close to the money wagon, which was what Longarm had come to think of Butler's private wagon.

Longarm reined the bay around and rode parallel to Johnson's leggy paint horse.

"Did you see anything?"

"Nope. Not a damn thing," Longarm said.

"Then what—"

"Like I said. I got a feeling."

"If you're wrong, then we will 've stopped this train for nothing. The boss won't like that," Johnson said.

Longarm nodded and reached for a cheroot, forgetting for the moment that he was out of smokes. "How will the boss feel if we ride into an ambush up there?" he said.

"Personally I'd rather give half a dozen false alarms than miss one real one an' let the boss get robbed."

Johnson grunted. "You aren't sure," he said.

"No. I told you that. But it feels . . . worrisome," Longarm told him.

Johnson pondered that for a moment. Then he nodded. "All right." He gigged his horse to the front of the train and held his hand up.

There was not room enough on or near the road for the wagons to be corralled, but they bunched up as best they could. Johnson and the other guards rode to the head of the train and pulled their Winchesters ready for action.

Longarm took the bay a hundred yards ahead of the train and reined to a halt there.

The forest crowded in on the road just ahead of the point where he stopped. He could not see anything, but once again he had the feeling that something was very definitely amiss.

That feeling was proven reliable half a minute later when the would-be robbers, apparently realizing their ambush was discovered, broke cover and came boiling out with their guns blazing.

There were seven of them, poorly mounted but well armed.

Longarm wheeled the bay horse and palmed his .45. He turned in the saddle, took careful aim while the attackers were still some distance ahead, and dropped two of the men with his first three shots.

His Colt barked again and a third man toppled out of his saddle.

Longarm fired his last two shots in rapid succession but hit no one with them.

He slapped the steel to the bay and headed back to the wagon train at a dead run.

As soon as he was out of the way, the other guards opened fire.

Whatever attackers remained lost their urge to fight. They turned tail and ran.

Longarm pulled in behind the lead wagon, shucked the empty brass out of his .45, and reloaded. Johnson came back to join him.

"That was nice o' you to hold fire 'til I was out o' the way," Longarm said.

"It seemed the least I could do." Johnson smiled. "Besides, I wouldn't want to lose that sensitive gut of yours. You really didn't see anything up there?"

"No," Longarm said, "nor smelled them nor anything else I could put a name to. It just . . . looked wrong, felt wrong."

"Well, I'm glad that you did. Incidentally, I intend to tell the boss what you did. I suspect there will be a bonus in it for you," Johnson said.

Longarm smiled. "I got to admit, money is the most sincere form of appreciation."

"Not that I can promise anything, but . . ."

"What do we do about the bodies o' those men I dropped up there?" he asked.

"If their pals didn't carry them off, we damn sure won't," Johnson said. "We'll drive right over them if they're laying in the road."

Longarm nodded. But when he resumed his post ahead of the train, he stepped off the bay long enough to drag the three dead men out of the road.

Chapter 50

They traveled for another three weeks, winding back and forth along country roads in northern Arkansas and southern Missouri, stopping every now and then for Howard Butler to buy more cheap whiskey. Longarm had not had any idea how prevalent moonshining was.

They stopped at so many places, many of them virtually hidden in the dense brush, that Longarm lost track of the locations. The best he would be able to do would be to give Mark Loomis a general idea of where to find some of the illegal whiskey makers.

Not that he was complaining. The cooks fed well. And he was still drawing his pay as a deputy although Butler and Johnson did not know that. His only distress was that he was out of his beloved cheroots and the only smokes he could find in the little mercantiles they passed were rum crooks—a poor substitute in his opinion.

They trended north and east, Butler obviously knowing where he was going, until eventually they reached the Mississippi River just south of Cape Girardeau.

Johnson approached him at supper that evening.

Longarm was seated on a crude bench with a tin plate of beef and beans in his lap.

"Normally," Johnson said, "you'd be laid off now that we've reached the river. But the boss says you're entitled to stay with the crew if you want to travel upriver with us. He figures he owes you for ferreting out that ambush a ways back. Do you want to stay on?"

Longarm pretended to think about the offer. He paused for perhaps ten seconds, then nodded. "I do, thanks."

"All right. The pay is the same, on the river or off. Work is the same, too. Keep your eyes open and your guns close. Which reminds me. You don't have a rifle, do you?"

"No, I don't," Longarm said. "Just my short gun."

"I'll get you one," Johnson offered. "If there's any trouble along the river, the shooting is likely to be at longer ranges."

Longarm grunted an acknowledgment and took a bite of biscuit. The head cook did himself proud with those biscuits.

"Come morning," Johnson said, "put your horse in the corral over there and pile your tack in the shed. They'll be there waiting for you when we get back."

"Someone will feed him?" Longarm said.

"Aye. He'll be tended properly."

Longarm doubted he would ever see the bay horse again, but that was Shorty's worry. And Shorty had more to worry about than an errant horse.

Chapter 51

The *Mary Ellen*—Longarm often wondered who Butler had in mind when he named her—was fifty some feet in length at a guess. She was a steam-driven sidewheeler, basically a flat-bottom boat with a steam engine perched amidships.

There was a pilot house where Howard Butler took his quarters. Everyone else stayed on deck along with the cargo.

Butler had the liquor transferred to the boat then paid off the drivers. Those individuals apparently owned their wagons.

It took most of the night to move the cargo aboard, then the drivers left. Butler kept his bodyguards on board, though.

True to his word, Johnson came up with a .38-55 Winchester for Longarm to use.

"Do you mind?" Longarm asked.

"Mind what?"

Longarm stepped over to the river side of the *Mary Ellen*, levered a cartridge into the chamber, and took aim at a piece of flotsam drifting past about seventy five yards out in the river.

He squeezed off a shot, the rifle smacking his shoulder with a satisfying push.

"Low an' a little to the left," he said aloud.

"You're not going to adjust your sights?" Johnson asked.

Longarm shook his head. "No need. I know where she shoots now. Better to adjust me than the sights."

"Suit yourself."

"Is the cook coming with us?" Longarm asked. "I do like what he puts out."

"Oh, yes. The boss would be lost without Jimbo," Johnson said.

"So would I," Longarm told the segundo. "I surely would."

As soon as all the whiskey and people were aboard, the three-man crew of the *Mary Ellen* got steam up and cast off from the quay.

"How far upriver are we goin'?" Longarm asked one of the crew.

"'Bout a thousand miles, give or take," the man said.

Longarm grunted softly. A thousand miles would put them into Indian country, just about where he expected Butler to go with his raw alcohol.

There must be one hell of a profit involved in this illegal trade, Longarm thought.

And very little likelihood that Howard Butler would be caught.

Longarm chuckled to himself. *Until now, that is.*

Chapter 52

"Shit," Longarm mumbled under his breath.

The stocky, flamboyant Indian who was approaching the *Mary Ellen* was Walks Far, a renegade Sioux whom Longarm had encountered before. The man was squat and stocky with pigtails down to his waist and a single eagle feather sticking straight up at the back of his head. He wore a beaded vest, bone gorget, and buckskins.

And Longarm did not like the son of a bitch.

They had been steaming north against the current for more than two weeks, tying up at night when the pilot could not see the cinkers that floated just beneath the surface of the river. Running into one of those could sink the craft. By now, Longarm suspected they were somewhere not far below Miles City.

Walks Far went into the pilot house with Butler. Longarm tugged the brim of his Stetson low and headed for the prow of the steamer, where he hunkered down behind a stack of crates that were headed north along with the illicit whiskey.

He had no idea what was in the wooden crates. They

were marked as farm implements, but he seriously doubted that. Something illegal, no doubt. After all, a man who would deal in alcohol would sell other items as well.

Guns? Longarm had been tempted to break into one of the boxes to see for himself but concluded he could do that after he arrested Howard Butler for selling whiskey to Indians.

In the meantime he needed to stay out of sight from Walks Far. And on a boat with no good places to hide, that might not be possible. Besides, if he made it obvious that he was trying to hide, he was bound to be exposed.

Better, he thought, to sulk here on the damp foredeck. If anyone questioned him, he could simply say he was in a lousy mood and please leave him alone.

Please. He had to remember to say please or risk getting into a brawl, and that would only call attention to himself, attention he most definitely did not want right now.

On the other hand, with the way he was feeling, he would welcome an excuse to haul off and break somebody's beak. His mood had been poor enough to begin with and was even worse now that Walks Far was aboard.

Longarm pulled out one of the detestable—but available—rum crooks, bit the twist rather savagely, and lit the cigar.

Chapter 53

What he needed, Longarm thought, was a stiff drink.
Which was funny, really. Here they were on a boat carrying several thousand gallons of raw liquor . . . and no one
was allowed to drink a drop of the stuff.

Of course, that made perfect sense. Give the men free
access to the liquor and there was bound to be trouble.
Still, just looking at the stuff made a man thirsty, never
mind that it was non-tax-paid booze. A man's gut cared
nothing about taxes and government regulations.

Longarm sat at the prow of the *Mary Ellen* and smoked
his cigar and hoped he could avoid being seen by Walks Far.

"Do you play?"

Longarm looked up to see a man named Elroy holding
a deck of cards.

"I said, do you play? Poker, I mean. Do you enjoy a
game of poker?"

"Oh, uh . . . no, thanks." The fact was, Longarm
enjoyed a game of chance as much as anyone and better
than most, but a game tended to draw onlookers. And

Longarm did not need a crowd for fear Walks Far would be included.

The bastard Indian threatened to ruin everything. And he did not even know it.

Longarm turned away from the friendly fellow and after a moment Elroy went aft to join the other guards.

That was only a temporary reprieve, Longarm knew. The damn boat was just not big enough to allow him to hide from Walks Far indefinitely. That being the case, he would just have to do something about it.

Longarm reluctantly got up and headed back toward the pilot house, where Walks Far had been the last time Longarm saw him. He was given a reprieve when the pilot steered toward the south bank, and Johnson called out, "Guards up!"

Chapter 54

Deckhands hurried ashore pulling hawsers to tie them to nearby trees. When no trees or rocks were available to anchor the ropes, the boat crew screwed iron corkscrews into the ground and tied off to those.

The crew was in charge during the day while the *Mary Ellen* was under steam, but Johnson's team of bodyguards took over at night when the boat was tied off to the land.

Longarm joined the others as they trudged ashore and chose positions where they could keep watch through the night, acting by turns. Longarm was paired with a man called Joyner. Neither of them was much for conversation, so they matched up well together. Apparently Johnson had noticed that and often paired them together for the all-night guard duties.

If nothing else, Longarm thought, the guard duty would keep him out of the sight of Walks Far.

Or so he thought.

"Long!"

Longarm stood, turned, realized with a start that it was Walks Far who had called him out. The Indian had come up behind him so quietly that Longarm had not heard the son of a bitch approach.

Now he was less than ten feet away and coming closer.

"What you—"

Before Walks Far could finish the question, Longarm launched himself at the man.

Longarm met Walks Far with a straight right hand that rocked the stocky Indian back on his heels. He followed the right with a tattoo of lefts and rights, digging into the Indian's belly and ribs.

Walks Far was taken aback by the sudden assault, but he recovered quickly and tried to grapple with Longarm.

Longarm was reminded that Indians wrestle and kick but rarely punch.

They do, however, tend to use their knives when it came to fighting.

Walks Far spun away from Longarm and reached for his belt knife, a wicked skinning knife that could eviscerate a buffalo, never mind the thin skin of a human being.

It was obvious the man had fought with steel before. He dropped into a crouch, protecting his knife hand with his left, weaving back and forth waiting for an opportunity to strike.

Walks Far's eyes were cold. He did not like Custis Long a bit better than Longarm liked him, and now that he had spotted Longarm, Walks Far intended to kill him.

Longarm's right hand leaped to the butt of his Colt. In the face of a man who was out for his blood, it was entirely reasonable that Longarm should drag iron and shoot the son of a bitch.

Still . . .

Longarm reached up and grabbed the brim of his Stetson. Moving in with the speed of a striking snake, he swept the hat into the face of his foe.

Walks Far jumped back, blinking and snorting.

Longarm moved quickly to his left and kicked Walks

Far's knife hand. Walks Far lost his grip on the haft of the knife and it flew high into the air.

When the Indian looked up to retrieve his knife, Longarm moved in, punching and kicking.

Walks Far threw himself at Longarm's legs. Longarm countered with a knee to Walks Far's face. He heard cartilage crunch as the tough Indian's nose broke, and blood began to stream down over his regalia.

Walks Far produced another knife—Longarm never saw where it had been hidden—and swept it upward toward Longarm's belly. Had it connected, Longarm's guts would have been spilled on the prairie soil.

It hit the buckle of his gun belt and turned aside.

Longarm threw himself onto the Indian, intent on smothering the other man's hands and arms. Instead Walks Far grunted in Longarm's ear, almost softly, and collapsed beneath Longarm's weight.

"Jesus," he heard Joyner say. "The red bastard stuck hisself."

Longarm stood, a little shaky after the brief but furious fight, to see the haft of the smaller knife sticking up from Walks Far's chest. The blade had been wedged between the two men. It pierced Walks Far's upper abdomen at an upward angle and must have plunged itself into the Indian's heart.

Walks Far was dead before anyone could rush in to pull them apart.

And before he could say anything about Custis Long and the badge he carried.

Chapter 55

"Boss wants to see you."

Longarm looked up to see Johnson standing over him with a rifle in hand. There was nothing unusual about that considering that they were there to protect the boss and the boat. And the weapon was not actually pointed at Longarm. But still . . .

"What about?" Longarm asked as he rose from the ground. He brushed himself off and picked up his own rifle. Johnson did not tell him to leave the weapon behind. Longarm took that to be a good sign. Perhaps he was not in that kind of trouble after all.

"This might surprise you, but the boss don't tell me everything. He just tells me what he wants, and what he told me he wants is you. Now hop to it," Johnson ordered.

Longarm was taken aboard the *Mary Ellen* and led into the pilot house. When they saw him enter, the captain and two crew members who were in the structure quickly left.

Howard Butler was sitting on a tall stool. He swiveled around to face Longarm. "You killed the Indian," he said.

"Yes, I did."

"I had the man aboard for a reason. Now you have managed to ruin that plan," Butler charged.

"Sorry," Longarm said, his tone of voice making it clear that he was not sorry at all. "We had history, him and me, though it's none o' your business what that history was. Fact is, if I hadn't killed him, he would've killed me. That's just the way it was. An' I wasn't gonna let him kill me just so your plans wouldn't be fucked up."

"I am not happy," Butler said.

"Yeah, well, I'm alive," Longarm said, "an' that makes me happy. I don't much give a shit if you like it or not."

"Now I have no interpreter," Butler said. "I could afford to lose a guard but not my interpreter. And I am not at all sure that I care for your attitude, Short."

"Tough shit," Longarm told his boss. "Now are you gonna fire me or can I go back t' my guard post?"

Butler hesitated. Then he said, "Go back where you were. I'll let you know if I decide to fire you." He hesitated again and added, "Although I get the impression it would be sensible to fire you instead."

Longarm turned without a word and followed Johnson back off the boat.

Chapter 56

"Did you hear?" Joyner said when he got back from chow shortly after midnight.

"Mm?" Longarm was half asleep, his eyes gritty and his mouth tasting foul.

"Two more days," Joyner said. "Rumor has it that we'll be there in two more days."

"We'll be where?" Longarm asked.

Joyner shrugged. "Who the hell knows. Somewhere in the middle of nowhere. Likely some creek or other where we can pull in out of the river. That way we won't be seen by any other boats passing by. Doesn't really matter where it is. The Indians will know."

"We're meeting a bunch of Indians?" Longarm said.

"Sure. What did you think? We're carrying a cargo of whiskey and guns, and those are the commodities the Indians want. What difference does it make to us anyway? Except . . . and this is the thing that puzzles me . . . what the hell would an Indian want with a Gatling gun?"

Longarm snapped wide awake. "A Gatling?"

"You know those crates up forward?" Joyner said. "I

know one of the deck crew, and he says two of those
crates hold Gatlings and half a dozen others are carrying
ammunition for the things. I mean, you can't hunt with
them. So what the hell would an Indian want with one?"

"You're sure about that? We're carrying Gatling guns in
the cargo to be traded?" Longarm sat up straight and began
to squirm.

If that was right about the cargo . . . no, one does not
hunt with a Gatling gun. But one could kill a whole lot of
United States soldiers with one. Give a single Gatling gun
to one of the wild tribes and teach them to use it, and they
could make Custer's massacre seem like a mere skirmish.
The bluecoats seldom marched with artillery. If the Indians had fast-firing ordnance like a Gatling gun, they would
be slaughtered.

"How many Gatlings? Did your friend say how many
we're carrying?" Longarm asked.

"He didn't say exactly. Just that we have some aboard.
That's what he said. Some. Like in, more than one. Do you
want me to ask him?" Joyner's voice turned suddenly
suspicious.

"No," Longarm said. "There's no need for that. I was
just curious, that's all."

The two were quiet for a spell, then Longarm asked,
"How do wild Indians pay for merchandise anyway? Does
the boss take trade? Furs or like that?"

"That will be the day," Joyner said. "He takes gold. Or
money. He'll take American money or British, but mostly
they pay in gold."

"Where would a wild Indian get gold?" Longarm asked.

Joyner shrugged. "They rob whites, I would guess.
There's a lot of miners up here who dig for gold. Then the
Indians come along and steal it from them, I think. The
way I understand it, they didn't used to pay much attention
to either the gold or the miners until Boss started up. And

he wants to be paid in gold. They want the whiskey and the guns, so they get it somehow."

"And the Gatling guns?"

"As far as I know, this is the first time we've ever carried those. Always before we were told we were selling guns so the Indians could hunt and feed their families. Now . . . I'm not so sure about selling Gatlings to them. Somehow that don't seem quite right. But then what do I know? I'm just a dumb bodyguard."

"Yeah, me, too," Longarm said. He feigned a yawn and settled back into silence.

But that did not mean he was not deep in thought.

Selling whiskey to Indians was illegal but probably not lethal.

Selling Gatling guns to them would be something quite different.

If it was true, Longarm could not allow it to happen. There was a hell of a lot more at stake than a simple arrest for whiskey peddling.

Chapter 57

"Short."

"Yes, sir."

"I want you to help Joyner make up the whiskey. He knows how so pay attention to the way he does it."

"Yes, sir."

Joyner came aboard the *Mary Ellen*. He looked tired. But then they had been awake all night on guard duty and now were expected to work through the morning, too. "Grab a bucket. I'll get some of those five-gallon tins."

"How do we—"

"I'll show you," Joyner said.

A gallon and a half of raw alcohol mixed with two gallons of water dipped out of the creek the boat was sitting in. A quart of molasses was added to that and a plug of tobacco was tossed in. Stirred all together, the combination made up the trade whiskey that they would sell to the Indians.

The whiskey was carried aboard in five-gallon tins, and they had a supply of extra tins sitting empty ready to be filled with the trade whiskey. And of course, as each tin was emptied of raw alcohol, it stood ready to be refilled with the crude whiskey.

At least, Longarm thought, there was nothing actually poisonous in the dark golden whiskey they made up in five-gallon batches.

Longarm and Joyner made up twenty gallons of the stuff. "That should do to begin with," Joyner said. "If we need more, we can make it then. Help me carry it over there, will you?"

They piled the tins of trade whiskey under one of the trees that lined the creek banks. On a hillside nearby Longarm could see a village begin to blossom and grow as Indians from several different tribes began to arrive and set up their tipis.

Children came to the creek bank to stare wide-eyed and curious at the white men and their boat. Women came to chase them away from the evil whites. But warriors came to sample the wares that the whites were offering.

"How does this work?" Longarm asked as he and Joyner began mixing a fifth batch of whiskey.

"The boss will hand out free whiskey for two or three days to get the Indians in the mood for some serious trade. Then when their appetite has been thoroughly whetted, he'll bring out the guns. And the whiskey, of course. We'll need a hell of a lot of the stuff for that last phase of the trade. Enough to keep the whole tribe drunk for a week or better. That way they'll think they got a good deal in the trading. They won't have any idea how bad they've been cheated." Joyner shrugged. "As long as they're happy with the deal, why not?"

"Yeah, why not?" Longarm said absently. But his thoughts were far from agreement.

"One more batch," Joyner said. "Then we can get some sleep."

"Right."

The boat crew left, apparently interested in finding

some Indian maidens to fuck, while the bodyguards set up a Sibley tent for Butler's use. Then they wandered off to find comfortable spots among the trees where they could stretch out and get a few hours' sleep.

"Coming?" Joyner asked.

"I'll be along," Longarm said. "I want t' line up some o' these tins so's we'll be ready when they need more whiskey."

"Suit yourself," Joyner said.

Longarm went up to the prow where the long crates were stored. He looked around and, seeing no one else aboard the *Mary Ellen*, pulled one of the heavy crates away from the others.

He entered the pilot house and found a pry bar then used that to open the crate. A brand-new brainchild of Dr. Richard Gatling lay there, packed in thick grease.

Longarm's heart began to race. The deaths of how many American soldiers—Canadians, too, for all he knew—lay there silent and deadly.

He had to find a way to stop this.

He replaced the lid on the crate then sat down to think.

He pulled out a cigar, nipped off the twist, and lit one of the last of his rum crooks. Once those were gone, it might be a while before he could find any more smokes.

Longarm flipped the spent match over the side of the boat and sat smoking for a minute.

Then he tossed his head back and laughed aloud. He knew what he could do to stop the Indians from getting the deadly cargo.

Chapter 58

Longarm whistled a happy tune as he went from tin to tin, pile to pile, stack to stack. His weapon to fight Howard Butler and his plan was nothing more complicated than his pocket knife.

The side walls of the whiskey tins were thin, which made them delightfully easy to puncture.

Longarm stabbed. And twisted. Stabbed and twisted. Stabbed. Twisted. And behind him the raw alcohol, some of it close to two hundred proof, gurgled and splashed, running down the sides of the piles of five-gallon tins, pooling on the deck, spreading to the gunwales of the boat and beyond.

And still Longarm stabbed and twisted.

Finally, with the deck of the *Mary Ellen* awash behind him, Longarm touched a match to the fumes rising from the spilled whiskey.

He heard a low whoosh and felt the bite of flame but saw nothing, the alcohol-fueled fire virtually invisible in daylight.

Longarm stepped ashore by way of the gangplank that

had been laid there and, still whistling, made his way to the spot where he had spread his blanket close to Joyner's.

Behind him he heard another, louder whoosh.

The flames were almost visible now. They engulfed the *Mary Ellen* from stem to stern but still there was no smoke. Above the boat, rising heat caused the nearby trees to seem to shimmer and dance.

Finally someone saw and raised the alarm.

Longarm, strangely enough, was not alarmed.

Besides, he was off duty now. He lay down and prepared himself to sleep.

Chapter 59

"Fire! Fire! Fire!"

Someone onshore noticed suddenly billowing flame and smoke and raised the alarm. By then the *Mary Ellen* was fully engulfed. Alcohol-fueled explosions had ripped through the boat, and the flames had begun consuming the wood of the craft. Once that began, the flames became visible and smoke rose dark and thick into the air.

People of all description began running at a furious pace toward the craft. Butler's crew of white men ran in an effort to extinguish the fire. The Indians, perhaps as many as two thousand of them, ran toward the scene so they could crowd close and watch. Indian children were underfoot everywhere. Men shouted comments and suggestions in half a dozen languages.

There were plenty of buckets. On board the *Mary Ellen*. The buckets burned, too.

Butler, aghast, actually tried soaking his coat in the creek and using the wet cloth to beat out the flames. It was a futile effort and more than a little stupid, which he quickly realized.

The boss stepped back from his blazing pyre of trade goods and wrung his hands. Longarm thought for a moment Butler was going to break into tears, and indeed he did wipe at his eyes a bit. But that might have been because of the smoke and soot in the air around him.

"All right, boys. Stand down. Let it burn," Butler said eventually, giving in to the inevitable.

And burn she did. Within half an hour the *Mary Ellen* was gone except for the paddle wheels, the stern boards, and some twisted metal that used to be a steam engine . . . and several crates of guns.

The heat had been fierce, enough so that the Gatling guns, when the scrap cooled and Butler was able to retrieve them, were warped and twisted, too. And completely unusable.

"We need horses," Butler told the Indian chiefs.

"What you pay with?" was their response.

"Lend them to me," he said.

"What you pay with?" was their response again.

Eventually the crowd of fascinated Indians wandered back to their own encampments, leaving the destitute whites to their own devices.

"I don't know what the hell we are going to do," Butler admitted to his assembled company of bodyguards and boat crew.

"Well, I do," the captain said. "I'm going to walk downstream to the Mississippi and signal the next passing boat to carry me down to Saint Louie."

That drew a chorus of *me-too*'s from the others.

Longarm went back to the place where he had laid out his blankets and fashioned a horseshoe roll much like the infantry carried back during the recent unpleasantness. He slung the roll over his shoulder and began walking along the bank of the nameless creek where the *Mary Ellen* met her untimely demise.

Soon enough the others began following.

Chapter 60

The small steamer, confronted with a dozen armed men onshore, quite sensibly stood off from the bank. The captain set a hook, picked up a megaphone, and called, "Who be you?"

Butler cupped his hands and responded in as loud a voice as he could muster. "Howard Butler and company here. We lost our boat to accidental fire. We need transportation to Saint Louis."

"I can take four of you aboard. I've no room for more," the captain of the *Jazzy Lady* called back.

"All right, but I need to reach the city as quickly as possible," Butler shouted. The man turned to his employees— or former employees, as it could well prove to be—and began pointing to one or another.

Longarm pushed his way forward and in a low, tight voice informed Butler, "I'm going along. Don't try an' keep me from it." His tone was frankly threatening and Butler acted like he had been slapped in the face.

Butler took half a step back and hesitated, then said, "Yes, fine, you can go. And you Johnson, Hitchcock, Tomlinson."

"That's five," Longarm pointed out. "The man said he'd take four."

"I, uh, you stay then, Tomlinson. Take charge here. Meet me in Saint Louis at Beardsden's."

Longarm had no idea who or what Beardsden's might be. And did not much care. Long before they reached Saint Louis, he expected to have Howard Butler in irons.

But he did not want to try taking the man down when he was surrounded by his bodyguards and by at least a thousand, probably twice that many, potentially volatile Indians.

"The ones who will come aboard stand apart from the others," the boat captain called. "Leave your weapons ashore. I will send a boat for you."

Sensible, Longarm thought. After all, the man did not know who or what this crowd might be. They could well be river pirates.

The *Jazzy Lady*'s crew muscled a small dinghy, no more than eight feet in length, into the water, and one man stepped into it. The others handed him a pair of oars and he set out for shore.

While the small boat was in transit, Longarm moved close to Butler, leaned down, and growled into his ear, "I'll go aboard first an' look things over for you."

Butler blinked, then said, "Yes. Yes, thank you. I hadn't thought of that." Apparently the man thought Longarm was still trying to protect him.

When the boat reached shore, Longarm stepped into it and sat at the prow. It took only a few minutes for him to reach the little steamer.

"I thought I told you no guns," the captain said.

Longarm pulled the man aside. Took out his wallet and flipped it open. "For your information only. Don't say anything to Butler."

"Who's Butler?" the captain asked.

"He's the asshole who's in charge back there. An' do you happen t' have any cigars aboard? I went an' ran out."

The captain looked a little confused. But he produced a box of panatelas, and Longarm very gratefully accepted one.

Chapter 61

"We'll be pulling into the quay at Saint Louis in a half hour or thereabouts," the captain announced.

"Can't you take us on to Cape Girardeau?" Butler said. "I could pay you."

"No, mister, I told you that a thousand times already"—an exaggeration but not much of one—"my bill of lading is for Saint Louis. Downriver to the Cape would cost me another day, day and a half and a good cord of wood, maybe more. No, sir, you get off at Saint Louis. You can get transport from there down to the Cape. Or swim for all I care."

"I said I could pay you," Butler insisted.

"Then you can pay someone else, and they can take you. Me, I'm pulling in right here." Captain Phillips looked at Longarm as if expecting the deputy to do something, but Longarm remained out of it. The truth was that it would be a convenience for him to get down the river to Cape Girardeau also. Saint Louis would certainly do, however. As soon as Butler was onshore again, Longarm intended to announce himself and make the arrest.

The crew warped the *Jazzy Lady* into the dock at the

riverfront quay and set about tying her up and laying a gangplank.

Longarm sidled up beside Howard Butler and took hold of the man's elbow. "I got bad news for you, Howard. You're under arrest."

"What the—"

"I'm a deputy United States marshal. An' you are shit outa luck."

"But you—"

Someone on the engine nearby opened a valve to take steam off for some reason Longarm would not have understood even if he had been told beforehand. The high-pitched screech and cloud of white steam startled Longarm. He looked aside to see what the commotion was. When he looked back again, Butler was halfway across the gangplank and running hard.

"Leave him," Johnson snapped, reaching into his pocket and producing a small nickel-plated revolver. Hitchcock, standing behind him, looked like he had not yet figured out what was happening.

"Don't do it!" Longarm warned.

Johnson raised his pistol and aimed it in Longarm's direction. It was a mistake.

Longarm swept his .45 into action. His first bullet took Johnson in the belly, his second in the chest. Johnson doubled over, turned half around, and pitched head first into the water between the boat's hull and the timbers of the quay.

Hitchcock, finally realizing at least some of the situation, clawed for his waist, apparently discovering to his horror that he had left his guns upriver when he came aboard the *Jazzy Lady*, and threw his hands up.

Longarm ignored the man and set off in hot pursuit of the fleeing Howard Butler, shouts of confused consternation in his wake.

Longarm caught a glimpse of Butler a block or so

ahead, racing through the city streets, dodging drays and carts and pedestrians. The son of a bitch could run, Longarm had to give him credit for that.

Longarm stretched his legs for all the speed he could muster. Slipped on a pile of fresh horse shit and ran into the back of a ponderous beer wagon carrying five massive kegs.

Butler ducked to the side, disappearing into an alley. Longarm followed, rounding the turn only to be confronted with the crack of a pistol shot and the droning zip of a bullet passing close by his head.

Longarm returned the fire, his bullet taking a chunk out of the shingled siding on someone's shop.

Butler stumbled, righted himself, and fired again. Longarm's answering shot went wide, leaving him only one more cartridge in his cylinder. And he could not very well stop to reload in the midst of a foot pursuit.

He did not need it in any event. Some citizen wearing a once white apron stepped out into the alley and ran smack into Longarm, knocking him off his feet. He fell onto a discarded crate holding rotted cabbage, bounced off, and surged back onto his feet.

He was too late. There was no sign of Butler ahead of him.

With a sigh, Longarm leaned against the side of the building, Colt still in his hand.

"Hey, mister, don't look at me like that," the poor fellow Longarm had run into quickly said. "I didn't do it a'purpose."

"Yeah. Right." Longarm flicked open the loading gate of his .45 and began shucking the empties.

Chapter 62

"Cap'n, what's the quickest way down t' Cape Girardeau?"

Phillips looked Longarm up and down. "Let me see that badge again, would you?"

Longarm nodded and pulled out his wallet. He let the boat captain inspect it to his heart's content, then the man said, "Downriver like that, going by way of a fast steamer with the current pushing you along, that'd be the quickest way down. And I just happen to know a man that has the boat for it. She's lean and fast. Won't hold much in the way of freight so he's always scratching for a dollar. If you pay him, he'd get you there about as fast as is humanly possible."

"Let's go see the man," Longarm said.

"You'd pay?"

"The United States government will pay."

Phillips nodded. "Let's go."

He led Longarm off the *Jazzy Lady* and two blocks up from the wharf. The saloon they entered was a dive, the sort of place where a man might not know if he was in for a drink or a fight. Or both.

"Joshua, this here is Deputy United States Marshal Long. I . . . what's your first name, Long?"

"Custis."

"Really?" Phillips's expression said he found the name remarkable, but he offered no remarks. "Anyway, Long, this is Captain Joshua Stone. He has about the fastest boat on the Mississippi. He can get you down the river quick as johnny-jump-up. Joshua, this man is willing to pay for a fast run down to the Cape. Do you have steam up?"

"Pretty much," Stone said. "She'd need to build some, but there still ought to be life in the boiler."

"How much do you want for the trip?" Longarm asked.

"How much freight are you carrying?" Stone asked.

"No freight, just me."

"And you'd be willing to pay what I ask just for you to get there?"

"I would."

"I come dear. And I'd have to give a little back to my friend Phillips here," Stone said. "A trip like that would be worth"—he paused for half a heartbeat—"twenty dollars, mister."

"Done," Longarm said.

He could see Joshua Stone mentally kicking himself as Longarm's ready acquiescence to the price suggested he would have paid even more.

"When can we cast off?" Longarm asked.

"Let me finish this beer and we'll be on our way."

Chapter 63

Longarm was reasonably sure he had reached Cape Girardeau ahead of Howard Butler. The question now was: Where would Butler go once he did get to the bustling river town?

Longarm had the entire trip downriver to ponder the question. The best he could do was take a guess. But that guess, he concluded, would be the livery barn where Butler stabled the group's horses. After all, at that time he expected to return, heavy with gold and ready to start thinking about his next trip north with whiskey and guns.

The thought of the wild tribes backed by roaring Gatling guns was enough to give Longarm cold shudders, and if Butler was low enough to try to deliver the fast-firing guns this one time, there would be nothing to stop him from trying it again.

Nothing, that is, unless his finances had been wiped out by the loss of his sidewheeler and that entire cargo. Longarm fervently hoped that the son of a bitch was now broke.

Regardless of the state of the man's finances, though,

Longarm intended to see that Howard Butler spent the next fifteen or twenty years behind prison bars.

He thanked Joshua Stone for the man's best efforts and paid him the promised twenty dollars, then stepped ashore on the Cape Girardeau wharf.

The livery that he wanted was only a matter of blocks away. Longarm smoked one of Phillips's panatelas on his way to the barn and tossed the butt away before he entered as some—most—stables were strict when it came to smoking indoors, where hay and dust combined to make fire a threat.

And Longarm had had quite enough fire lately. He could not suppress a smile, though, at the thought of the *Mary Ellen* engulfed in flame.

"Something you need, mister?" the hostler asked when he got there.

"Waitin' for someone if that's all right. He'll meet me here direc'ly," Longarm said.

The hostler nodded and went back to mucking out one of his stalls.

Longarm chose a comfortable-looking pile of hay in the loft and settled down to wait for Howard Butler to show up.

Chapter 64

Longarm awoke from a light doze. From his bed of straw in the loft above, he heard voices below. He had been inside the barn continuously for a day and a half save only time to go find a meal or take a shit. Now . . . one of the voices sounded like Howard Butler's. And there was the hostler. And a third voice that he did not know.

He crept forward to the edge of the platform and peered down. The third man was no one he knew.

Butler, Longarm noticed, was wearing a revolver now. And acting like the big shot again. Never mind the disaster up north, Butler had his swagger back. Probably had a fat bank account here in Cape Girardeau, Longarm guessed. Or someone willing to back him in another attempt to get illegal whiskey and guns to the Indians.

Either way, the son of a bitch was on his way to a Federal cell now.

Longarm checked to make sure his .45 was positioned where it should be then stepped onto the ladder.

Howard Butler's look of shock when he saw Longarm was enough to put a smile on Longarm's face.

"Like I mentioned before, Howard, you're under arrest," Longarm said. "An' you gentlemen, please stand aside while I put some irons around Howard's wrists."

The hostler quickly backed away, holding his hands out to show he was offering no resistance, but the third man, heavyset and swarthy enough to suggest he might have some Indian or Mexican blood in him, went for his pistol.

Longarm's gun was quicker. His .45 barked once, twice, and the heavyset man went down, bleeding and no doubt hurting but probably not dying from the punctures in his flesh.

While his chum was standing and fighting, Butler was ducking, out of the way and out of sight inside one of the stalls.

Longarm stepped over to the heavyset man, knelt down, and picked up the revolver he was no longer interested in using, his concentration at the moment having shifted to the likelihood of his own survival.

"Lay still," Longarm told him. "You'll make it."

The fellow looked at him and grimaced but gave a faint, hopeful nod. He had a hand clamped over the wound in his side. The other was on the point of his shoulder. Neither should be life threatening.

Satisfied that he was not going to be shot in the back when he went after Butler, Longarm stood. He stuffed the wounded man's Remington .44-40 behind his belt and took a moment to reload his .45. Now that he was trapped inside the horse stall, Howard Butler was not going anywhere.

"You might as well give yourself up, Howard," Longarm said, raising his voice to make sure the bastard heard.

"Who the hell are you, Long? Is that even your real name?" came a response from inside the stall.

"I told you, Howard, I'm a U.S. deputy marshal, an' I'm placin' you under arrest. We'll go over all the charges when I get you back t' Springfield, but I reckon you already know what most of 'em will be. You're just makin' it worse by resisting so drop your gun an' come out easy."

"You'll shoot me if I do," came the response.

"Howard, I'm gonna shoot you if you don't. Now come outa there."

There was silence for several minutes, then the stall door swung open.

Still Butler did not emerge.

Longarm heard a horse snort and only then realized that Butler was not the only occupant of that stall. There was a horse in there, too, and Longarm could well imagine the use Butler would try to make of the animal's size and speed.

He stepped back to the side so he would not be trampled when Butler came bursting out on or running beside the horse.

On? Or beside?

Longarm put his money on "beside." The man would want the bulk of the horse to shield him from Longarm's bullets.

More silence. More shuffling of feet. Getting up his nerve? Longarm suspected that would be the cause of the delay.

Still he waited, his Colt held ready.

Then in a rush the horse bolted out of the open stall door into the alleyway down the center of the barn, heading for the open back and freedom.

Butler had one fist clenched in the gray horse's mane and was half running, half dragged along by the sudden burst of speed from the gray.

Longarm snapped a shot beneath the horse's belly, hoping to get a lucky hit on Butler's legs.

He heard a scream and Butler let go of the mane. He fell and his shield galloped on without him.

Butler lay on his left side. He held a pistol in his right hand and was still moving.

Longarm shot him. Paused to take careful aim and shot him again. The second bullet struck Butler in the nuts and ranged upward through his body cavity, poking holes in things everywhere it went.

"Let go of the gun," Longarm ordered.

Butler did not comply, so Longarm shot him a third time while he lay on the ground, this slug striking his belly and again plowing upward, shattering his heart and putting an end to it.

Even so, Longarm's approach was cautious until he could kick the pistol safely out of Howard Butler's hand.

He made sure Butler was dead, then turned back to tend to the wounds of the heavyset fellow.

"You can come back now," Longarm called to the hostler. "Go get a doctor for this man an' tell the local law what's gone on here. Oh, an' I'll be needing me that bay horse. I have t' take him back to Springfield."

He smiled at the thought of what else lay in Springfield. It would be good to see Jenny again. Maybe take a few days of vacation before he headed back to Denver. He wondered if Jenny might enjoy a little trip down to Hot Springs to take in the baths there. And other things.

And his smile grew even wider.

Watch for

LONGARM AND THE STAGECOACH ROBBERS

the 433rd novel in the exciting LONGARM
series from Jove

Coming in December!

LONGARM

GIANT-SIZED ADVENTURE FROM
AVENGING ANGEL LONGARM.

BY TABOR EVANS

penguin.com/actionwesterns

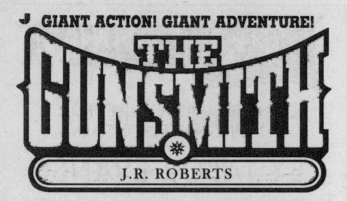

GIANT ACTION! GIANT ADVENTURE!

THE GUNSMITH

J.R. ROBERTS

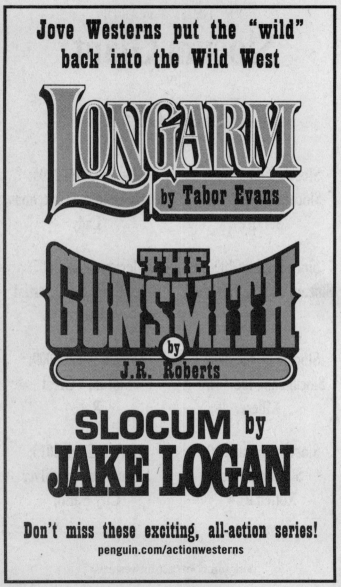